WHEN MY NAME WAS KEOKO

Linda Sue Park

A DELL YEARLING BOOK

Published by
Dell Yearling
an imprint of
Random House Children's Books
a division of Random House, Inc.
New York

Visit us on the Web! www.randomhouse.com/kids

Educators and librarians, for a variety of teaching tools,
visit us at www.randomhouse.com/teachers

ISBN: 0-440-41944-1

Reprinted by arrangement with Clarion Books

Printed in the United States of America

January 2004

OPM   10 9 8 7 6 5 4

To my children:
SEAN AND ANNA

❦

and for my parents:
EUNG WON / NOBUO / ED
JOUNG SOOK / KEOKO / SUSIE

Acknowledgments

Heartfelt thanks to Audrey Debije, Marsha Hayles, Patrick O'Neill, Ed and Susie Park, and Nancy Quade, for reading drafts of the manuscript and offering valuable comments; Ginger Knowlton, for cheering me up and on; Jim Armstrong, for his eagle eye; Ben Dobbin, for constant support; and especially Dinah Stevenson, for clearsightedness, gentle prodding, and timely doses of encouragement over what proved to be a long haul.

A note on Korean terms of address

Terms of address are an important part of Korean culture. In addition to relationship, they signify rank, respect, and affection to a greater degree than their equivalents in English. The following terms of address are used throughout this story:

Abuji (ah-boo-JEE): "father"

Omoni (uh-muh-NEE): "mother"

Hyungnim (hyung-NIM): "older brother," used by a younger brother

Opah (OH-pah): "older brother," used by a younger sister

Ajima (ah-JIM-ah): "auntie," used for relatives and also as a term of respect and affection for older women outside the family

Yobo (yuh-BO): like "dear" or "honey," used exclusively between husband and wife

I have taken the liberty of using "Uncle" instead of the correct Korean term, *Ajushi*, because I felt its similarity to the word for "father" (*Abuji*) might cause confusion for readers.

1. Sun-hee (1940)

"It's only a rumor," Abuji said as I cleared the table. "They'll never carry it out."

My father wasn't talking to me, of course. He was talking to Uncle and my brother, Tae-yul, as they sat around the low table after dinner, drinking tea.

I wasn't supposed to listen to men's business, but I couldn't help it. It wasn't really my fault. Ears don't close the way eyes do.

I worked slowly. First I scraped the scraps of food and dregs of soup into an empty serving dish. Then I stacked the brass bowls—quietly, so they wouldn't clang against one another. Finally, I moved around the table and began putting the bowls through the little low window between the sitting room and the kitchen. The kitchen was built three steps down from the central courtyard, and the sitting room three steps up. From the window I could reach a shelf in the kitchen. I put the bowls on the shelf one at a time, arranging them in a very straight line.

The longer I stayed in the room, the more I'd hear.

Uncle shook his head. "I don't know, Hyungnim," he said, disagreeing respectfully. "They're masters of organization—if they want this done, you can be sure they will find a way to do it. And I fear what will happen if they do. Our people will not stand for it. I am afraid there will be terrible trouble—"

Abuji cleared his throat to cut off Uncle's words. He'd noticed me kneeling by the table with the last of the bowls in my hands; I was listening so hard that I'd stopped moving. Hastily, I shoved the bowl through the window and left the room, sliding the paper door closed behind me.

What rumor? What was going to happen? What kind of trouble?

When I asked Tae-yul later, he said it was none of my business. That was his answer a lot of the time. It always made me want to clench my fists and stamp my foot and hit something.

Nobody ever told me anything. I always had to find out for myself. But at least I was good at it.

You had to do two opposite things: be quiet and ask questions. And you had to know *when* to be quiet and *who* to ask.

When was easy. I was supposed to be quiet most of the time. The youngest in the family was never supposed to talk when older people were talking. And girls weren't supposed to talk much anyway, not when men or boys were around. So listening was easy for me; I'd done it all my life.

But lots of times I didn't learn what I wanted to know by listening. That was when I had to ask questions.

I could have asked my mother, Omoni, when we were doing housework together. But I'd learned that it was useless to ask her most questions. Either she didn't know the answer or she wouldn't tell me. Men's business, she'd say.

Abuji knew almost all the answers. I was sure of that. But I hardly ever asked him. He always said exactly what he wanted to say, and no more.

That left Uncle and Tae-yul. Usually, I tried Uncle first. He was quite cheerful about answering me most of the time. And when he wasn't around, I'd ask my brother. First-born son, only son—the men usually included him in their talks.

Tae-yul was thirteen, three years older than me. He was often impatient when I asked questions, and acted as if I were stupid for asking in the first place. But that was better than not knowing things.

Listening and asking weren't enough, of course. After that came the hard part—the figuring out.

They'll never carry it out. . . . They're masters of organization. . . . I knew who "they" were. The Japanese. Whenever there was talk that I wasn't supposed to hear, it was almost always about the Japanese.

A long time ago, when Abuji was a little boy and Uncle just a baby, the Japanese took over Korea. That was in 1910. Korea wasn't its own country anymore.

The Japanese made a lot of new laws. One of the laws was that no Korean could be the boss of anything. Even though Abuji was a great scholar, he was only the vice-principal of my school, not the principal. The person at the top had to be Japanese. The principal was the father of my friend Tomo.

All our lessons were in Japanese. We studied Japanese language, culture, and history. Schools weren't allowed to teach Korean history or language. Hardly any books or newspapers were published in Korean. People weren't even supposed to tell old Korean folktales. But Uncle did sometimes—funny stories about foolish donkeys or brave tigers, or exciting ones about heroes like Tan-gun, the founder of Korea. Tae-yul and I loved it when Uncle told us stories.

3

We still spoke Korean at home, but on the streets we always had to speak Japanese. You never knew who might be listening, and the military guards could punish anyone they heard speaking Korean. They usually didn't bother older people. But my friends and I had to be careful when we were in public.

Every once in a while another new law was announced, like the one when I was little that required us to attend temple on the Emperor's birthday. I decided that this must be the rumor—Abuji and Uncle had heard about a new law.

I was right.

2. Tae-yul

Sun-hee is a real pain sometimes. Always asking questions, always wanting to know what's going on. I tell her it's none of her business, which is true. Abuji would tell her if he wanted her to know.

But *I* don't know what's happening either. Why hasn't he told me? It's not like I'm a little kid anymore—I'm old enough to know stuff.

One day I get home from school and Uncle comes in right after me. He's early, it's way before dinnertime. He's got a newspaper in one hand, and he walks right past me without even saying hello. "Hyungnim!" he calls.

Abuji is in the sitting room. Uncle goes in and closes the door behind him. I listen hard, but I can't hear anything— until Uncle raises his voice. "I won't do it!" he shouts. "They can't do this—they can't take away our names! I am Kim Young-chun, I will never be anyone else!"

Omoni and Sun-hee come out of the kitchen and look at

4

me. I turn away a little, annoyed that I don't know what's going on. Just then Abuji opens the door and waves his hand toward us. So we all go into the room. Uncle is pacing around like crazy.

Abuji reads out loud from the newspaper: "'By order of the Emperor, all Koreans are to be graciously allowed to take Japanese names.'"

"'Graciously allowed . . .'" Uncle says. His voice is shaking, he's so mad. "How dare they twist the words! Why can't they at least be honest—we are being *forced* to take Japanese names!"

Abuji reads some more to himself, then says, "We must all go to the police station in the next week to register."

Uncle curses and pounds his fist against the wall.

My name, Tae-yul, means "great warmth." My grandfather—Abuji's father—chose it. It's one of our traditions for the grandfather to do the naming. He'd taken it seriously, Omoni once told me; he'd wanted a name that would bring me good fortune.

For Sun-hee, too—"girl of brightness."

A different name? I can't imagine it. I look at Sun-hee and I can tell she's thinking the same thing.

"Those who do not register will be arrested," Abuji says.

"Let them! Let them arrest me! They will have my body but not my soul—my name is my soul!" Uncle's face is red as a pepper.

Abuji holds up his hand. "Such talk is useless. It must be done. But let me think a while."

We leave him alone. I'm last out of the room, but I don't close the door. I watch him take a few books from the cupboard and turn the pages. Then he gets up again and fetches

5

paper and pencil. Writes something on the paper, looks at it, writes some more. What's he doing?

At last he calls us all back into the room. Sun-hee and I sit on the floor, but Uncle stays standing, his arms crossed. Stubborn. Abuji waits a few moments, until Uncle seems calmer and uncrosses his arms.

"Tae-yul, Sun-hee, you know that the Kim clan is a large and important one," Abuji says. "Long ago, all Kims lived in the same part of Korea, in the mountains. Choosing the word for gold as their name shows what a strong clan they were. Gold was only for kings."

He picks up the sheet of paper from the table and points at it. "I have chosen our Japanese name. It will be Kaneyama. '*Yama*' means 'mountain' in Japanese, and '*ka-ne*' means 'gold.' So the name will honor our family history."

He turns to Uncle. "*They* will not know this. But we will."

Uncle doesn't look so mad now. "Kaneyama," he says quietly, and bows his head. "Hyungnim has chosen well."

"As to our first names," Abuji says, "Sun-hee, fetch your primer."

Sun-hee goes to the cupboard and brings back an old book. I know the book—it was mine first, then hers. The Japanese alphabet is on the first page. Abuji takes the book and opens it.

"We will close our eyes and point. Whatever letter we point to, we will choose a name that begins with this letter. These are not our real names, so we do not care what they are."

Uncle grins. "That's very good, Hyungnim. In fact, I do not care at all—you may choose my letter for me."

Abuji smiles, too. "No, we will each choose for ourselves."

6

First Abuji, then Uncle. My turn. I close my eyes, point my finger any old way, and then look.

N. My new initial.

My new name: Kaneyama Nobuo.

3. *Sun-hee*

That night in bed my thoughts were racing around in circles. I was remembering something that happened when I was only six years old.

Four years ago the Olympics took place in Europe. It was so exciting. My family crowded around the radio each night to hear about the competitions. Tae-yul and the other older boys made hurdles in the lane. My friend Tomo and I ran races with each other. We threw long sticks and pretended they were javelins. We even built an Olympic stadium.

Building cities was our favorite activity. In the vacant lot down the lane from my house we'd gather up stones, sticks, little bits of wood. We used them to build cities—houses, schools, shops, a marketplace, a temple, army barracks. Sometimes we built a train station and tracks, too. We used long sticks for the rails and broke other sticks into shorter lengths to make the crosspieces.

We always had long discussions as we designed and planned our cities. Sometimes we'd build for days, then stop, take everything apart, and start over again.

I remembered the stadium especially well. It was so different—oval instead of square; we'd heard about it on the radio, its strange shape and how big it was. The stadium had been one of our greatest successes. For days we had races inside it, using little stick people as runners.

7

On the last day of the Olympics, we all gathered as usual to listen to the radio. And as usual, Uncle translated the announcer's words for Omoni.

Omoni knew a little Japanese, but not enough to understand the broadcast. She could speak only Korean, because she'd never gone to school. Back in the days when she was growing up, most girls didn't go to school.

The rest of us knew Japanese. Tae-yul had learned in school, like Abuji and Uncle. At the time I wasn't old enough for school, but I'd learned to speak and understand it from my friend Tomo. We'd been friends since we were babies.

Because of the way Uncle translated, I was glad I could understand Japanese. The announcer described the scene, the noise of the crowd, the colors of the athletes' uniforms, and how they were lined up on the track. But Uncle would just say something like, "The hundred-meter race is beginning." He never translated the details, but Omoni didn't seem to mind.

Now Uncle listened to the announcer for a few moments, then turned to Omoni. He said, "Instead of a baton, the French relay team will be passing one of those long loaves of bread."

Of course the announcer never said any such thing; Uncle was making it up. Tae-yul snorted, and I hid a smile behind my hand. Omoni rolled her eyes doubtfully.

"No, no, it's true," Uncle insisted. "It's a national symbol for them—they obtained special permission from the Olympic Committee to use it. The committee said yes, but each time a runner receives the handoff he must take a bite of the bread." He acted it out for her—pretending to receive a bread-baton and then taking a bite of it while running.

Tae-yul and I laughed. Even Abuji smiled. Omoni covered

8

her face in embarrassment at being teased, but I could see that behind her hands she was smiling.

After the relay the broadcaster announced that the marathon runners would be entering the stadium soon. Uncle looked at us excitedly. "There's a Korean runner in the marathon," he said. "He's one of the best in the world—he has a very good chance at the gold medal."

We all leaned a little closer to the radio.

"*. . . the first runners should be entering the stadium at any moment now. . . . They will make their way through the entrance tunnel and emerge onto the stadium track for a final lap. . . . In a moment or two we should be able to see the leader. . . . There he is now! It's Kitei Son! Kitei Son of Japan—*"

Uncle reached for the dial and turned it off abruptly, then slammed his hand against the radio so hard that he knocked it over. I stared at him with my mouth open. Everybody sat there, frozen.

Uncle jumped to his feet, his fists clenched by his sides. I'd never seen him like that before.

"Kitei Son!" he said, his voice trembling with rage. He spat on the floor, as if the name tasted bad. He choked out, "That is not his name." And with that he left the room.

I looked at Abuji and Omoni. Their faces were very serious. I waited, hoping one of them would explain. But when Omoni finally spoke, it was only to tell us to get ready for bed. Abuji said nothing at all.

Nobody explained why Uncle was so angry. I went to bed feeling cross and worried.

The next morning Tae-yul waved at me to come out to the back garden. He looked solemn and important, the way he always did when he knew something I didn't.

"Uncle talked to me," he said in a low voice. "The man

who won the marathon—Kitei Son? He's the Korean runner Uncle was talking about. His real name is Sohn Kee Chung."

"So? Why did that make Uncle angry?"

Tae-yul shook his head impatiently. "Sun-hee, don't you understand? People all over the world know about the Olympics. He'll be in all the newspapers—"

"That's good, isn't it? He'll be famous!"

"He was wearing the *Japanese* flag on his uniform. The newspapers will give his *Japanese* name. No one will know he's Korean—they'll all think he's Japanese. . . ."

This is what I was remembering the night we all chose our new names. New for *us*, but the Japanese had renamed people before.

I only meant to remember that much, the part about Sohn Kee Chung's Japanese name. But remembering isn't something you can stop doing just because you want to. My mind kept going even though I tried to turn it onto another path. I saw Uncle's face floating above me in the darkness: covered with bruises, his lip split and bleeding.

It's all right, I told myself firmly. *He's all better now.*

4. Tae-yul

Kaneyama Nobuo . . . Kaneyama Nobuo. No matter how many times I say it, I can't get used to it. It feels all wrong, like shoes that don't fit.

On the way to bed after we get our new names, Sun-hee whispers to me. "Sohn Kee Chung," she says, her eyes big.

I nod—I've been thinking of him, too. The Olympic champion. A world record holder in the marathon. The

10

newspapers call him Kitei Son. But Uncle always calls him by his Korean name.

The day after the Olympics marathon, Uncle doesn't come home for dinner. After we eat, Abuji goes out. He doesn't say where he's going, and he's gone a long time.

We're in the sitting room. It's late, past bedtime, but Omoni doesn't seem to notice the time. We hear someone coming, and I run to the door.

Abuji comes in with his arm around Uncle. Holding him up, sort of dragging him. Because Uncle can hardly walk.

He's been beaten up. Really bad.

Omoni bathes Uncle's wounds and bandages them, with him groaning the whole time. Sun-hee gets in the way, so Omoni sends her to bed. I help Omoni, fetching water and rags.

Abuji talks to me afterward.

"My brother was at his shop late today because he was waiting for the newspaper delivery." I know that newspapers from Taegu, the nearest city, get delivered to Uncle's printing shop late in the day. "There was a photograph of the marathon champion on the front page."

A pause. He looks away from me. "Uncle and some of his friends changed all the newspapers. They crossed out the Japanese name and wrote his Korean name in its place. They altered the Japanese flag on his uniform, too—they drew a wavy line in the middle of the circle, so it looked like the Korean flag instead."

I gasp. So brave of Uncle! He must have known he could get into trouble. But he did it anyway. "What happened?" I ask. My voice comes out all croaky. I take a breath, steady it, speak louder. "How did he get hurt?"

"They were caught in the act by a group of soldiers and dragged off to jail. All of them were beaten. Besides his face, he has several broken ribs. They kept most of them in jail, but a few were released."

"Why? Why did they let them go?"

"I am not sure. Perhaps as a warning. They want the townspeople to see them, to see how badly they have been hurt. To discourage further acts of this sort." A pause. "Or perhaps out of respect for my position at the school."

We're quiet for a little while. Then Abuji tells me to go to bed. "Sleep by your sister tonight," he says.

Sun-hee's eyes are closed, but she isn't asleep. When someone is really asleep they look . . . I don't know, heavier. Anyway, I can tell she's still awake.

And probably scared. She's only little. I get out some bedding and lie down right next to her. I whisper, "I know you're still awake, Sun-hee. Don't worry. Uncle is hurt, but he's going to be all right." I don't know that for sure, but I'm hoping hard. If he was worse, Abuji would have gone for the doctor.

Sun-hee turns toward me and touches my arm. I let her take my hand and hold it until she falls asleep.

A few days later Uncle calls Sun-hee and me into his room. It's the first time we've been allowed to see him. I've been sleeping in my parents' room to let him rest quietly.

He's still hurting a lot. It's hard for him to move or even take a deep breath. The swelling on his face has gone down, but the bruises look awful. Dark blue, purple, red, and the biggest one, on his cheekbone, is greenish yellow around the edges.

Uncle sees the way I look at him. He grins and makes a

terrible face. That makes me feel a little better. Then he tells Sun-hee to bring him the mirror. She holds it in front of him.

"Oh! Such colors!" he says. "Really, they're rather pretty, don't you think? I wonder if I could manage to stay this way."

We laugh and I feel even better. He always makes us laugh.

Then Uncle nods at me. "Paper and pencil," he says.

What for? I get them from the shelf and give them to him. He raises himself up on one elbow, wincing. Then he takes the pencil and draws a rectangle on the paper.

"I am going to draw the Korean flag for you," he whispers.

I lean closer. There have been rumors in the street, people talking about Sohn Kee Chung and the newspapers. But I hadn't seen the paper. The Japanese had burned them all. I'd never seen a Korean flag either.

Uncle draws a circle in the middle of the rectangle.

Sun-hee pouts. "That looks just like the Japanese flag," she says. I'm thinking the same thing. It's the flag on top of every public building in town: a red circle on a white ground. So familiar.

"Shh. Wait." Uncle draws a curved line in the middle of the circle. "The top half of the circle is red"—pointing with the pencil—"and the bottom is blue."

Then he draws four symbols, one in each corner. "These are black," he says. "Each has three parts, and each part represents a different cycle. The seasons: summer, autumn, winter, spring"—he points at the corners in turn. "The directions: south, west, north, east. And the universe: sky, moon, earth, sun."

"That's good, Uncle," Sun-hee says, bobbing her head and smiling. "It's a lot fancier than the Japanese flag."

Uncle smiles back at her. Then he looks serious. He glances around cautiously, so I do, too. Only the three of us there, but I still get a funny feeling, like someone might be watching us. "Bow," he whispers. "Bow to the Korean flag."

We stay as we are, squatting on our haunches, but we bow our heads.

"Never forget," he says. "Keep it in your minds always— what the flag looks like and what it means."

His voice is quiet, but strong at the same time. I stare hard at the paper, trying to memorize the flag.

As usual, Sun-hee has a question. "Why, Uncle? Why do we have to remember it? Why can't we just put the picture up on the wall? That way we'll see it every day and we'll always know what it looks like."

Uncle reaches out and pulls gently on one of her braids. "We can't, little cricket. It is against the law to fly this flag— even to put up a picture of it. Korea is part of the Japanese Empire now. But someday this will be our own country once more. *Your* own country."

He looks at us again. "You have it now? In a safe place in your minds?"

Sun-hee nods so hard her head is like a bouncing ball. I just look at Uncle and nod once.

Uncle lies back down. "Burn it," he says.

Sun-hee looks scared. She follows me to the kitchen. Omoni is out doing the marketing. I wonder what she'd think if she were here.

We watch the drawing blacken and then disappear in flames. Sun-hee looks a little less scared then.

When we get back to his room, Uncle raises his head and stares at both of us. "Never forget," he says again. "I swear there will come a time when you, little Sun-hee, will sew that flag. And Tae-yul, you will help put it up over every building in the land."

His words put a picture in my head. Me, on the roof of a building, raising a big Korean flag. Uncle down below, signaling to me that the flag was straight. It'd be fun, climbing on all the roofs.

There will come a time . . . he'd said.

But when?

5. Sun-hee

When we chose our new names, I pointed to the letter *K*. I went around whispering over and over, "Keoko. Kaneyama Keoko. Keoko."

Kaneyama: Japanese family names were usually long.

Kim: Korean ones were short.

Keoko: Japanese first names could be long or short.

Sun-hee: Korean first names were almost always two syllables.

I'd always liked the sound of Japanese first names. "Tomo" meant "friend." I remembered learning that when I was little. It had pleased me so much that my best friend's name was "friend"! His sisters were Sachiko and Hiroko. Girls' names often ended in "ko," which means "girl" in Japanese.

I liked how Abuji had hidden our real last name in the new one he'd chosen for us. And he'd done the same for my first name as well. "Ko" meant girl, but it could also mean "the sun's rays." Rays of brightness, the same meaning as my real name.

15

I could think about "Kaneyama Keoko" as a name but not as *my* name.

For the next few days, there was terrible confusion at school. We had to learn our classmates' Japanese names and call them by those names. Suddenly, the girl across the aisle from me was Megumi, not Myung-gin. And the boy who sat behind me was Masado instead of Young-won. In school, when I spoke of my brother, I had to call him Nobuo!

Our teacher tried to be patient with us. If we forgot and used our classmates' *real* names, she prompted us—gently at first, but more sternly as time went on.

I was a good student; I'd never once given the teacher cause to beat me. I was very careful to use everyone's Japanese name and to respond when anyone said "Keoko," even though it felt as if they were talking to someone else. But on the second day of the name change my brain grew tired of being careful every single minute, and I called a classmate by her Korean name.

I chose the worst possible moment to make this mistake. Onishi-san was in the room. He was the man who served as the military attaché for our school. Our teachers were Korean, but their bosses were Japanese. Onishi-san's job was to make sure all the students were learning to be good citizens of the Empire.

He came into our classroom several times a week, often in the middle of a lesson. We always stopped what we were doing and bowed to him. Then he'd stand at the back of the room and observe us for a while. I could tell he made the teacher nervous. I tried especially hard to give the right answers when he was around.

16

That day, I *knew* he was in the room. I knew I had to be extra careful not to make a mistake. And somehow I did the very thing I was trying so hard not to do—I said "Myung-gin" instead of "Megumi."

Onishi-san heard me. He made a funny sound in his throat, like "Ah!" Then he looked at the teacher and made an abrupt motion with his stick.

The teacher glanced at him quickly and then at me. "Keoko! To the front," she said.

The class was suddenly silent. I could see the surprise in the faces of the other students. The daughter of the vice-principal—who had never before been beaten . . .

In the brief moments it took me to walk to the front of the class, I saw the teacher's face. She looked so unhappy that I felt sorrier for her than for myself. She didn't want to beat me, but she had to—because Onishi-san was there.

It was so unfair. First our names were taken away, and then we weren't given even a few days to learn everyone's new name.

So when the bamboo cane swished through the air I was angry, not frightened. With each stinging whack, the word rang in my mind . . . *unfair—unfair—unfair—unfair—unfair*. . . . Best of all, I was too angry to cry.

At home that night Omoni pressed her lips together when she saw the fierce red welts on my legs. She soothed them with a paste made of herbs, but the marks stayed there for several days. I was glad they didn't fade right away. Seeing and feeling the sore redness of those welts always made me a little angry all over again.

I wanted to stay angry about losing my name.

———

The changing of my name made even Tomo cross. When we played together after school during those early days of the name change, he kept catching himself. "Sun-hee—I mean, Keoko," he kept saying.

Once, after correcting himself for what seemed like the hundredth time, he stamped his foot in frustration. "Keoko-Keoko-Keoko," he said, as if trying to pound the name into his brain. "Keoko-Keoko-Keekeeko-Kekoko—" He was getting his tongue all twisted.

I giggled. "Kee-kee-ko? Ke-ko-ko?"

"Ke-ya-koo! Ko-ko-ka!"

Now we were both laughing.

"Ka-koo-ko!"

"Ke-ay-ka!"

Tomo was laughing at the silly sounds. I was laughing for the same reason, but I was also secretly pleased to be treating my Japanese name with such disrespect.

At last our laughter faded and we caught our breath. Tomo glanced at me quickly, then looked away again. "Maybe, when it's just the two of us alone, I could still call you Sun-hee. What do you think?"

It wasn't often that Tomo asked for my opinion. I wanted to answer carefully, so I thought for a moment. "Wouldn't that just make it harder?" I said. "You'd have to switch to my Japanese name when we're with other people. You might get mixed up and—and forget."

I didn't say all that I was thinking—that as the son of the principal, Tomo always had to set an example. A mistake from him would be worse than a mistake from other students; he would lose a lot more face. I didn't have to say it, because it was something Tomo lived with every day.

18

"You're right," he said. He flicked another glance at me. "It's such a nuisance, isn't it?"

And I knew this was his way of saying he was sorry I had to change my name.

It was our last year of school together. Elementary students all went to the same school, but in junior high, boys and girls went to separate schools.

Not that Tomo and I saw each other much in school anyway. The Japanese students had their own classrooms. Tomo had told me that in bigger cities the Japanese had their own *schools*. But our town was too small for that.

I only saw Tomo at assembly times, which were in the morning, when the whole school met in the courtyard to recite the Emperor's education policy. We also sang the Japanese national anthem and did exercises together. And once in a while there were special assemblies.

Even though I couldn't read Japanese when I first went to school, knowing how to speak it made all the lessons much easier for me. At the start of my second year I was made Class Leader because I was the best in my class at reading and writing.

We had to learn three kinds of writing. Two kinds used the Japanese alphabet, and there were two different alphabets. The third system, which most of my classmates found terribly difficult, was called *kanji*.

Kanji has no alphabet. Instead, each word is a separate picture-character. Altogether there are nearly fifty thousand characters! Not even scholars who spend their whole lives studying kanji can learn them all. We had to learn about two thousand basic characters—to recognize them in reading and to write them ourselves.

We had calligraphy lessons as part of studying kanji. I loved calligraphy the very first time I tried it. It seemed that an unknown creature came to life in the brush as soon as I picked it up—a creature light as a dragonfly, smooth as a snake, quick as a rabbit.

The combinations of kanji characters were like magic to me. For example, the character for "love." You wrote the character for "mother" and combined it with the one for "child." When stroked with the brush rather than sketched out with a pencil, the word truly did look more loving.

Every week we learned new characters. Sometimes the connections were easy to understand. The character for "life" was formed by writing "water" plus "tongue"—for without water to drink there can be no life. The characters "rice" and "mouth" together made "happy" or "peaceful." It was true—how could you be happy or at peace if you were starving?

Kanji was full of secrets like this. Tae-yul hated studying kanji; he thought it was boring. I couldn't understand that at all. Maybe I loved kanji because it was about knowing a little and figuring out the rest.

Abuji noticed my interest in kanji and began to spend more time with me. Before, Omoni had always looked after us; Abuji was busy with his own work. Until he started to help me study kanji, I'd spent very little time with him.

My lessons in school concentrated on learning and memorizing characters. This was so difficult and took so much time that the teachers didn't explain much about each individual character. Abuji took my learning a step further—or rather, a step backward.

One night we sat together at the low table in his room, bent over a sheet of paper.

"Mouth," he said as he wrote the character: ☐ "This is very simple. It began as a circle, like an open mouth, but the line was squared to make it easier to combine with other characters.

"West. As the sun goes down, the birds fly back to their nests. So you see—" and he drew for me the progression of pictures that had evolved into the character for "west."

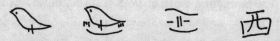

I loved these sessions with Abuji. I watched with my eyes and listened with my ears and learned with my heart. My kanji got better without it ever feeling like work.

At the end of my fourth year of school I was awarded a special prize for my language skills. All students wore two badges on their collars, one with the school's name and the other with their graduation year. I was given a third badge to wear. It meant I was the best in my grade at Japanese. It was the proudest moment of my life when the principal pinned the badge to my collar in front of the entire school. I didn't look at Abuji, but I could feel how proud he was.

As I left the platform to rejoin my class, Tomo smiled at me with his eyes. I was so surprised and pleased that I almost stopped walking. Tomo and I never talked to each other at school. Even when I did see him—in the courtyard before school or during assemblies—I pretended I didn't know him, and he did the same with me. It was just the way things were: Japanese and Korean children didn't mix during school.

Tomo must have noticed my surprise, for he quickly looked away. But that didn't bother me. Nothing could have bothered me as I walked back to my seat. I felt as if I were floating on a bright rosy cloud.

That afternoon on my way home from school I felt something whiz past my ear. I turned around quickly, ducking just in time as a second pebble flew past. I kept my head down but glanced around wildly. Who was throwing stones at me?

At that moment a gang of boys from school dashed out from behind a wall. They threw a final volley of pebbles at me, then ran away, chanting: "*Chin-il-pa! Chin-il-pa!*"

Chin-il-pa meant "lover of Japan." It was almost like a curse. *Chin-il-pa* were people who got rich because they cooperated with the Japanese government. I hadn't done anything like that! Why were they cursing me, calling me that awful name? I ran home, blinking away tears.

That evening I was distracted during my kanji session with Abuji. He was showing me "north"—two men sitting back-to-back at the top of the world—as I stared not at the paper but at the shining new badge on my collar.

The badge was the reason those boys had thrown stones and called me names. I was good at Japanese. They thought that made me *chin-il-pa*. I wasn't a traitor, was I? Could you be a traitor without knowing it? Even to be called one was shameful.

Maybe I could take the pin off. But they'd all notice—my teachers, the principal, Abuji, everyone. Then I'd be in trouble at school as well.

I tried to make myself laugh inside by recalling Uncle's favorite joke about the *chin-il-pa*: "They eat Korean rice, but their poop is Japanese." But not even this cheered me.

Suddenly, Abuji put down the pencil and looked at me thoughtfully.

"You know, Sun-hee, kanji was not originally Japanese."

Not Japanese? What did he mean? I looked up at him, puzzled.

"Both Korea and Japan long ago borrowed the system of character writing from China. The Japanese use it in their own way, of course, especially when they combine it with their alphabetic writing. But the characters are the same. This"—he picked up the pencil again and pointed to the page—"is the character for 'north' in Japanese *and* in Chinese. And in Korean as well."

Abuji stacked the books neatly, rolled up the paper, and put away the ink pot. I stood and bowed to him, preparing to leave the room.

He spoke again. "Your grandfather was a great scholar. He knew much of the important classical Chinese literature. In his time and for hundreds of years before his time we Koreans always considered Chinese the highest form of learning." He paused and looked at me calmly. "To excel at character writing is to honor the traditions of our ancestors."

I hadn't realized that my worries were showing on my face, but Abuji had noticed. What he'd said was meant to comfort me and to make me feel proud inside myself again.

I nodded, hoping he understood my silent thanks. If those boys called me *chin-il-pa* again, I could reach inside and hold on to the knowledge he'd given me.

6. Tae-yul (1941)

Abuji and Sun-hee spend hours studying kanji together. I sit with them sometimes, but I can't figure out why they think it's so interesting. Kanji is a complete bore.

I do my best in school, but really I hate it. Not that

23

I'm a bad student. I always know my lessons. Son of the elementary-school vice-principal—it would be shameful if I did poorly. But I've never been Class Leader either.

Abuji doesn't scold me about my grades. When I was younger, I used to wonder about it, why he didn't get angry with me. Surely he *felt* angry. He was such a good scholar, just like his father. Both of them had been Class Leaders their whole lives. Whenever I show Abuji my marks, he always looks disappointed. But he never yells at me.

Science and mathematics lessons aren't too bad. But we study those subjects for only a little while each day. Most of the time we study Japanese. Japanese and more Japanese. And kanji is the worst of all.

Each word is a separate character, and some characters look alike. A single brushstroke makes the difference between "sky" and "big." Two characters close together often make a whole new word. Who thought up this stuff? They must have tried on purpose to make it confusing. I spend hours studying kanji, until the strokes and lines look like one big blur on the page.

Sun-hee actually *likes* kanji. When she first started school, she asked for my help. But pretty soon she got really good at it. Now she knows as many characters as I do. More, probably.

We study together every day after school. One day I throw my pencil down on the table. "I can't stand it anymore," I say, gritting my teeth. I feel like shouting, but Omoni's in the kitchen; I don't want her to hear.

"What's the matter, Opah?" Sun-hee asks.

"Kanjikanjikanji all day long—that's what's the matter. I'm sick and tired of staring at these stupid characters."

She frowns. "They're not stupid."

I roll my eyes at her. "You wouldn't understand."

"You're right," she says. "I don't understand. I like studying kanji."

"What's there to like about it," I grumble.

I don't mean it to be a real question, but she answers anyway. "It's a story. Every character is like a story."

"A story? What are you talking about? A character can't be a story, not by itself. You have to have a whole bunch of them to make a story."

"The characters don't make the story, Opah," she says. "*I* do. Look—"

She writes down some characters. But first she sort of takes them apart, so you can see how they were formed. I've watched Abuji do this when the three of us study together, but I haven't paid attention like she has.

Then she points to the characters one by one.

口 "Mouth," she says.

門 "Gate.

問 "When you put them together, you get 'ask' or 'question,' right? It's a guard at the palace gate, and he's questioning Sim Chung's poor blind father—you know, the part where he almost gets turned away, but she recognizes him just in time."

Uncle has told us that fairy tale lots of times, but it's not like the gate is a big important thing in the story. I don't know how she comes up with these ideas.

25

"The story helps me remember," she continues. "Look, here's another.

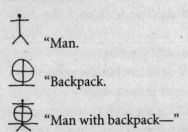 "Man.

"Backpack.

"Man with backpack—"

"—and then you sort of square off all the lines to get 'heavy.' This man's been on a long trip, and his backpack is full of silk and jewels, lovely things for his family—"

I flap my hand at her impatiently. "You think like that for every character?" I say. "That's crazy, you'll never remember them all."

"No, Opah, it makes it *easier* to remember them. Shall I show you some more?"

"No thank you!" I almost shout. She looks hurt for a moment, then presses her lips tight shut.

I sigh and go back to my own work, wishing for the thousandth time that kanji had never been invented.

I study what I have to, to pass my classes. Then I slip out to our workplace—Uncle's and mine—under the eaves at the back of the house. A workbench and shelves for our tools.

Ever since I was little, I've liked mechanical stuff—things that move. Uncle once made me a top. You spun it, then kept it going by whipping it with a string on a stick. My friends and I had contests to see who could keep their top going the longest. I was good at it—I won nearly every time. The trick was in the timing. Whipping it at just the right moment to get it going really fast.

That's what I like best: speed.

The Japanese military have cars. And motor scooters. Sometimes I stand by our front gate, waiting. Sooner or later a car or scooter drives past. First the sound, from far away. Then—*whoosh*. My hair and clothes swishing as it goes past. So fast!

Someday I'll have a scooter of my own. And then a car.

For now, I have a bicycle. Or what will be my bicycle someday. Right now it's just part of an old bicycle that one of Uncle's friends threw away. It's in really bad shape, with only the frame and chain worth saving. But everything else we can put together ourselves. Eventually—I mean, it'll take time to get everything we need. And I can't work on it as much as I want.

Sometimes when I go out to the work area, by myself or with Uncle, Abuji comes out, too. He watches for a little while, not saying anything. Maybe he wants to help. But he isn't good with his hands. Not like Uncle.

And Abuji being there always makes me feel guilty. Like I should be studying. Uncle feels it, too. He always says we've done enough for today, and I have to go back inside.

Still, I'm getting a lot done. I cleaned all the rust off the frame and repainted it. Then I made handlebars from lengths of pipe, pedals from sheet metal, a seat from a piece of wood. It took me a long time to whittle the wood into the right shape.

Now I have to figure out how to pad the seat. Then the bike will be finished except for the tires. Uncle told me not to worry about the tires. He'd take care of them somehow. But that was over a month ago. He's been working late at his printing shop, so we've hardly had any chance to work on the bike together. I check the rubbish heaps in town every day, hoping someone might throw out an old tire. But I never see one.

Omoni helps with the seat—a cloth cover and straw padding. The cover is sort of a drawstring bag. The string loosens so the bag will fit over the seat and the straw, then pulls tight and ties underneath. I sit on the seat and jiggle around. The straw slides out of place a little but stays inside the cover.

One day just before dinner, I'm trying to study. Uncle shouts from outside, "Nephew! Get out here, you lazy dog—am I supposed to do all the work myself?"

I jump to my feet and rush out the door. Then I stop, halfway down the path.

Uncle is coming through the gate. He's rolling one bicycle tire ahead of him. With a second around his neck like a giant rubber necklace.

Uncle isn't tall like Abuji. He's short and sturdy. He looks so funny—that tire around his neck hanging way down past his waist.

I laugh at first. Then I let out a shout and run to meet him.

7. Sun-hee

It wasn't fair. Why couldn't girls ride bicycles? It wasn't like the old days when girls had to wear long skirts. Omoni still wore long skirts, and so did a lot of older women. But young women and girls like me wore trousers. Omoni had told me it was the Japanese who had brought in this style. A lot of people hadn't liked it, but I couldn't understand why. Trousers were much easier to wear, and better for playing in.

I could have ridden a bicycle. It didn't look that hard. Tae-yul fell off a few times when he was first learning, but it wasn't long before he was able to wobble around the outer courtyard, and then up and down the lane. By the third day he was so good at it that he took off to ride around town, and I couldn't even watch him anymore.

When I turned to walk back up the path to the house, I stumbled on a little stone and twisted my ankle. I crouched down and rubbed the sore spot, then stood up and kicked the stone with my other foot as hard as I could.

The stone went skipping down the path; I watched it until it slowed down and finally rolled to a stop. Not like Tae-yul on the bicycle. He wasn't very good at stopping; he always slammed on the brakes and fell off.

I went in to help Omoni with dinner. Abuji was listening to the radio. He and Uncle listened a lot these days. There was a war in Europe, and a lot of news about a German leader named Hitler. It didn't really interest me—a strange-sounding name from a place I knew little about.

When I heard it was just war news on the radio again, I went into the kitchen. It was my job to prepare the rice every evening. I looked in the rice barrel. Empty. I was finding it empty more and more often these days.

It was because of the war, but not the one in Europe—the one in Manchuria. Japan was at war there, fighting against the Chinese. This was why they'd taken over Korea in the first place; it was only one step from the northern border of Korea into Manchuria.

29

The Japanese army always needed supplies. For years they'd taken part of every rice crop to send to the troops in Manchuria or to ship to Japan. Sometimes there was no rice in the marketplace; other times it was very expensive. To make it last longer, Omoni had started mixing it with barley.

Barley was cheaper than rice. We thought of it as food for poor people. It was chewier and coarser and had a strong flavor. Neither Tae-yul nor I liked barley; we used to pick out the brownish grains and eat only the rice.

But soon there was more barley than rice in our bowls. We couldn't pick it out anymore—there would've been hardly anything left to eat. I guess you could say we got used to it, but there were still times when I missed having a whole bowl of pure white rice.

It seemed we'd be having only barley tonight. I picked up the barley bag and was startled by how light it was. There wasn't enough for a meal. "Omoni—" I started to ask.

"Here," she said, handing me another bag. I opened it and looked inside.

It was millet. Little round yellow grains that farmers used as chicken feed. Startled, I looked up at Omoni again, and she nodded reassuringly. "It's quite nutritious," she said. "Who knows, perhaps it will even make a nice change."

I said nothing. I could hardly believe we were cooking animal food for our dinner.

As usual I served Abuji, Uncle, and Tae-yul their food first. Tae-yul took one look at the yellow grains in his bowl and said, "Omoni, what's this?"

It was very rude of him to comment on the food at all, and even ruder to ask such a question of Omoni. Abuji looked at him sternly. It was Uncle who answered.

"That's millet, nephew. Come, now—chickens and pigs love it, so I'm sure it will be good for you too!"

Uncle smiled at Tae-yul and took a big bite. "Your mother is such a good cook, she can make even millet taste delicious. Now, then, eat when you are eating, talk when you are finished." That was one of our traditional sayings; it was good manners to pay full attention to your meal.

Uncle's words had been said in his usual cheerful joking manner, but there was a hint of a warning behind them. I heard it, and I knew Tae-yul did, too, for he ate his dinner without another word.

Millet had a grassy taste and felt awful in my mouth—half mushy, half crunchy. I never got used to it, even though we had it nearly every day from then on. The bowls of yellow grain made me long for rice even more.

But Omoni always made our meals taste better by cooking lots of vegetables—squash, sweet potatoes, cucumbers. She was a skilled gardener, and the vegetable patch flourished no matter what the weather.

I liked helping her prepare the bed—chopping and crumbling the dirt until it was like silk between my fingers, then planting the seeds or seedlings in nice straight rows and giving each of them a drink. And later in the year I loved it when she'd tell me to run out to the garden and gather vegetables for our dinner. But I hated weeding and often found an excuse to be doing something else when Omoni went out to weed.

Along the back of the vegetable patch was a row of small trees. Really, they were more like large shrubs. In the summer they blossomed—big pink- or white-petaled flowers with magenta throats. They were rose of Sharon trees, the

31

national tree of Korea. Omoni had planted them years before, when she and Abuji had first moved to this house.

One evening in the fall Uncle brought home more news. The government had issued another official order. All families who had cherry trees were to dig up shoots and saplings from around their trees and bring them to police headquarters. The little cherry trees were to be planted all over town, and everyone was supposed to take good care of them.

The government order spoke of wishing to make our land more beautiful, with thousands of cherry trees. But it wasn't just a wish for beauty. The cherry tree was a national symbol of Japan.

And the final part of the order was that all rose of Sharon trees had to be uprooted and burned. The military police would be inspecting gardens to see that the order had been followed.

Omoni stayed inside the house; she couldn't bear to watch as Tae-yul chopped down the rose of Sharon trees one by one and dug out their roots. It was a difficult job; the trees were old and their roots reached deep into the ground. I helped him by dragging the fallen trees to a corner of the yard, where they'd be burned later.

Tae-yul had reached the last tree—a small one that Omoni had planted only a few years before. As he began to dig, Omoni came out of the house and said, "Tae-yul, wait. First go fetch a big pot, or a basin or something."

"What kind of pot?"

"I don't know—it needs to be big. Oh, wait—where you keep the tools, there's an old ceramic pot, with a crack in it. That will do."

I helped Tae-yul carry the pot out to her. It was quite large, as large around as my two arms could make a circle.

"Now," Omoni said, pointing to the last little tree. "Dig in a circle, and be careful not to cut any of the roots. I want you to bring the whole root ball out of the ground."

This took a long time. Tae-yul had used an ax to chop up the roots of the other trees and make it easier to dig them out. Now he could only use the shovel. Omoni returned to the house, but she came out from time to time to watch him work.

At last he put down the shovel and wiped his brow. "I think I can get it out now," he said. Although it had been the smallest tree, it was nearly as tall as me. Tae-yul pulled it carefully out of the hole and laid it down on the ground.

"Omoni!" I called.

She came out again and patted Tae-yul's shoulder. "You did a good job," she said. She walked around the little tree. "I think you will need to cut off about this much—" She pointed to a spot about a third of the way down from the top.

While Tae-yul chopped away with the ax, Omoni took up the shovel and began to fill the ceramic pot with dirt from where the trees had been dug up. Now I knew what she was doing. I got a trowel from the tool shelf and helped scoop dirt into the pot.

Omoni and Tae-yul lifted the little tree and settled it into the pot. Then we packed more dirt and mulch around it. Finally, I fetched a basin of water and gave the tree a drink.

The three of us stepped back and looked at the tree and then at each other. We were tired and dirty, but we managed to smile. We'd hardly spoken throughout the entire task, yet we'd all known what to do. It felt good to have done this together.

All the same, I was troubled: Omoni was breaking the law. If she got caught—if the guards discovered the little tree—

what would happen? Would she be arrested? A cold wind blew through me.

I was afraid for her. But I was proud of her, too. How could I be proud of my mother for breaking the law? I shook my head, trying to clear it of these confusing thoughts, and looked at Omoni again.

She was watching as Tae-yul lifted the heavy pot onto an old burlap sack. There was something in her face I hadn't seen before.

I didn't often think about what my parents looked like. They looked like my parents, that's all. But sometimes when she was sitting calmly, sewing in the pale light near a window, I could see that Omoni was pretty. Her face was more round than oval, but she had lovely clear skin. She wore her long hair braided and coiled in a neat bun at the nape of her neck. Sometimes at night when she took it down, she let me brush it. I loved doing that. My own hair had been cut short, chin-length with bangs, when I started school, because that was the required hairstyle.

Each of Omoni's eyelids had a delicate fold in it. This was unusual, and it was considered a trait of luck and beauty. My eyelids had folds, too. Because of them, and maybe because I was a girl, I thought I looked more like Omoni than Abuji. Tae-yul was just like Abuji, both of them tall and thin.

Now Omoni had a firm expression on her face, almost stubborn. Maybe she was afraid, too—but she wasn't letting it show.

Tae-yul dragged the sack and pot across the garden to the house. He paused and looked around, then put the tree in its pot near the tool shelves.

"There's plenty of stuff here," he said. "If we need to, we can put things over the tree to hide it."

I looked around anxiously and saw a few old sacks in the corner. I picked them up and draped them carefully over the tree. Tae-yul took a rotten straw basket and some pieces of wood and leaned them against the pot. It was a good disguise—the tree now looked like a pile of old junk.

"Good," Omoni said and smiled at both of us.

Later that afternoon the soldiers came around to inspect our yard. I was weeding in the vegetable garden and held my breath as they walked around.

For a few minutes they stood and watched Tae-yul at work burning a huge pile of rose of Sharon trees. Then they nodded at each other and marched off.

I let out my breath in a whoosh. The little tree in its pot amid the workshop clutter was safe.

Omoni took even better care of the little tree than she did the garden. Once I heard her murmuring quietly as she pruned it, when she thought no one was around. "The time will come," she said to the tree, "when you will be free to grow in a place of honor. I will see that you live until then— that is a promise."

Truly, rose of Sharon trees are not as beautiful as cherry trees. But if that little tree were ever planted outside again, I knew it would be the most beautiful tree in the world.

8. Tae-yul

It's a good thing Uncle and I have so much junk stored in our work area. That makes it easier to keep the little tree hidden. Uncle often brings home broken pieces of machinery, old tools, other odds and ends he finds at work.

Uncle's business is a print shop. He does mainly advertisements. Flyers, signs, things like that. Most of his customers are

Japanese. He says that's because the Japanese control the banking system. Koreans can't get loans. When a Korean business fails, it has to be sold, nearly always to a Japanese buyer.

Uncle is polite to almost everyone. But I can tell he wishes he had more Korean customers.

Every day after school I stop by Uncle's shop, hoping he'll need help. I tie up flyers with twine, make deliveries to customers, even just watch while he works.

Used to be, he wouldn't let me stay. He'd send me home to study. But on my bicycle I get to his shop really fast. Lots faster than walking. I told him how much time the bike saves me, and that I can spend the extra time in his shop. He laughed at me. But now he sometimes lets me stay a while.

My favorite times are when he runs the press. I help with setting the type, inking, making sure the paper runs through like it's supposed to. I love the sound of the press when it's running, that steady rhythm. And seeing the printed pages come out at the end, the ink all wet and shiny.

Even better is when the press breaks down. Not that I *want* Uncle to have trouble with it. But it's an old press and has a lot of problems. I like helping him work out what's wrong and then find a way to fix it.

Dinnertime, a month or so after the business with the rose of Sharon trees. Uncle is excited about something. I wonder if he'll talk about it after the meal. Millet again. But at least there are beans in hot sauce to go with it.

Uncle does talk to Abuji after the meal. I sit back and listen.

"I had a visitor at the shop today," Uncle says. "Lim. We did some talking."

I wonder who Lim is. Abuji doesn't ask—he must know already.

"Lim thinks it would be a good idea for me to expand my business," Uncle continues, "to encourage customers with deeper pockets."

Abuji says nothing, just raises his eyebrows a little.

"I think I'm going to take that advice," Uncle says. "It's been slow lately. And certainly *some* customers can afford to pay well." He picks up his cup for one last gulp of tea and waits for Abuji to say something.

I think I know who Uncle's talking about: Japanese customers.

At last Abuji leans forward, serious. "Be careful," he says. Then he gets up from the table. Conversation over. I don't know why Abuji said that to Uncle, but the way he said it worries me.

After that things are different at the shop. Uncle changes, almost overnight. He *welcomes* business from the Japanese merchants. Works long hours to get their orders finished ahead of schedule. Offers them special bargains—fancier designs for their flyers, a greater quantity for the same price.

Some of this stuff I overhear when he talks to Abuji. Other things I see for myself when I stop by the shop. Uncle, being very friendly with his customers. Joking with them instead of serving them quietly like before.

It takes only a few months for his business to grow. A lot. But I'm not glad about it—I'm worried.

Uncle being friends with the Japanese businessmen . . . I hate what I'm thinking. But I can't stop thinking it.

Uncle, *chin-il-pa?* Making his business more successful by favoring the Japanese?

Not possible.

But what else could explain the change?

———

37

Uncle is the younger brother. His duty is to obey Abuji. Before, they almost never disagreed with each other. But now things are different.

Uncle stays late at his work, sometimes coming home after dinner. Then they argue.

Omoni shoos Sun-hee and me out of the house so we can't hear. When we come back in, Uncle is grim-faced, Abuji silent, their words like ghosts hanging in the air.

One evening when we're sent out of the house I creep around toward the back, toward the room I share with Uncle. There's a paper window in the wall.

Just then Sun-hee calls out to me. "Opah! What are you doing?"

I wave her away. But she does something pretty smart— she waits until I've almost reached the window. Then she tiptoes after me. I can't yell at her now, they'll hear me. So I just glare at her and put a finger to my lips.

We crouch there together and listen.

"You show great disrespect by not heeding my desires." Abuji's voice is stern and sad.

"Hyungnim, please try to understand," Uncle says, pleading. "You are the firstborn. Your duty is to the family. You cannot do as I know you would wish to do, were the circumstances different. I am a second son. I have no wife, no children. It is men like me who must act on behalf of our people. How can showing love for our country be considered dishonorable?"

Abuji again. "A second son's duty is also to his family. What if something were to happen to me? Is it not a second son's responsibility to keep the good of his family always foremost in his thoughts and deeds? You put yourself in danger. That is a great disservice to the family."

"But is it not for the good of my family—for every family—for our entire nation—that I act as I do? Hyungnim, I do not wish to anger you. But I tell you now, I will not stop what I am doing. If it is your wish, I will leave the house so your orders will not be disobeyed in your sight. That is all I can offer."

Silence. Sun-hee looks at me, her eyes wide. But at least she knows not to talk.

I can hardly believe it myself. But I know why Uncle said it. Saving face—Abuji's face. If Uncle doesn't listen to Abuji, his older brother, it makes Abuji look bad. With Uncle living somewhere else, Abuji wouldn't know what's going on. So he wouldn't be as responsible. I hold my breath, waiting to hear what Abuji says.

We hear the sound of the paper door sliding open. One of them is leaving the room. Which one?

Then Abuji's voice. "This is your home." The door slides shut again.

That's it. Argument over. I still don't understand, but I know Uncle will stay.

I tiptoe away from the house. Sun-hee follows me. Any minute now, she'll start asking questions. We reach the back garden, and right away she says, "What's Uncle doing, that Abuji wants him to stop?"

I shake my head. "I'm not sure. But it must be dangerous somehow, or Abuji wouldn't be worried."

She has her hands on her hips, glaring at me. "Are you telling the truth? Or are you saying that because you think I won't understand?"

I'm trying to figure things out—I don't have time to answer a million of her questions. I take a deep breath, hold it for a moment, and let it out. "No, Sun-hee, really I don't know. But at the end there, Abuji sort of said it was all right for Uncle to keep doing what he was doing. I don't know what that is, honest."

She looks doubtful for a moment longer, then nods. "Maybe you and I could figure out what it is. Maybe we could help."

I've got the same idea. About myself, anyway. She's only a girl—how could she help? But right now I have to get rid of her so I can think. "Good idea, Sun-hee. You come up with a plan, and I will, too, and we'll get together and talk things over, OK? You be sure to tell me if you ever find out anything."

Her eyes bright. "Yes, Opah." She goes back into the house.

Good. Being nice to her worked. I go to the workshop area, pick up a rag, and begin polishing my bicycle. My hands moving by themselves, my thoughts on Uncle.

Uncle becoming *chin-il-pa*—is this what worries Abuji? The *chin-il-pa* do everything they can to please the Japanese. Patriotic Koreans—those who work for independence from Japan—hate the *chin-il-pa*. Sometimes the patriots wreck shops and homes. There are rumors that *chin-il-pa* get beaten, even killed. Abuji's face always goes dark when he hears those rumors. Koreans killing Koreans, he once said— it's worse than anything the Japanese can do to us.

Maybe that's why they argue. Abuji is worried about Uncle. That makes sense.

But then I think about Uncle telling us those old Korean stories, and how he hates having to use a Japanese name. How he'd shown us the Korean flag, and what he'd said just now, about our country.

40

There's no way he could be *chin-il-pa*—I'm almost certain about that.

Almost.

9. Sun-hee

It wasn't easy to think of a plan when I didn't even know what the problem was. Uncle was doing something that Abuji didn't like. So should the plan be to try to stop what Uncle was doing? Or to help him do—whatever it was, and then get Abuji to agree that it was a good thing?

At least I knew what the first step was. I needed to find out exactly *what* Uncle was doing. So I started stopping by the shop on my way home from school.

I didn't think Uncle would suspect anything; I'd always gone to his shop at least once every few weeks. If he wasn't too busy, we had fun together. He'd print fake newspapers with my name in them. Like the time I'd been named Class Leader. "Kim Sun-hee Appointed to Important Post"—that's what the headline had said.

Of course I couldn't keep the papers because he always used my Korean name. So I'd look at them for a while and then burn them. It was odd, but whenever I had one of those pretend newspapers in the house, my hearing seemed to get better. I was always hearing footsteps in the lane—footsteps that sounded like Japanese guards.

The first time I went to Uncle's shop on my "mission," it was a bright autumn day. My friend Jung-shin came with me.

Jung-shin's family had moved to town some months earlier, and we'd become friends almost right away. I liked her on sight, because she had the same kind of smile behind her eyes that Uncle did.

We had a lot in common. We were both the youngest in our families—she had an older sister, Hee-won. Both of us liked to read and enjoyed learning kanji. We were exactly the same height. And her Japanese name was Keiko, which was very similar to Keoko.

Jung-shin was teaching me to play cat's cradle. Every day she brought a long piece of string to school. She'd tie the ends of the string together and put her hands into the loop. Then she cleverly wrapped and pulled the string with her fingers until it looked like a gate with crossed bars. She showed me how to transfer the string from her hands to mine in another pattern. We passed the string back and forth; Jung-shin seemed to know dozens of ways to make new patterns with it.

I made up little stories to go with the passing of the string and would say them aloud:

"A girl opens the gate—" (the crossed bars)

"—and she comes to a road." (the string in four neat straight lines)

"The road goes over a bridge—" (crossed bars like the gate, only upside down)

"—on which a spider has woven its web."

This was my favorite pattern; it was intricate but perfectly symmetrical and really did look like a spider's web.

We always played cat's cradle for a few minutes after school. Sometimes Jung-shin would come home with me. We'd do our homework together, and then play more cat's cradle.

Jung-shin was better at it than I was—she played quite

often with her sister—and when we played fast it was almost always my fault when the string ended up in a tangle. We passed the string so quickly that we had to concentrate hard on making the right moves, and it was always a relief to collapse in laughter when one of us made a mistake.

That was how Jung-shin's sister, Hee-won, usually found us, playing cat's cradle or else silly with laughter. On the days Jung-shin was at my house, Hee-won often came by in the late afternoon to walk her home.

On this particular day I had had enough of cat's cradle and thought of something else to do. "Let's go into town," I suggested. "We can find the popcorn man."

A few days earlier Jung-shin had brought me a special treat—a few pieces of *duk*. This sweetened rice cake was my favorite snack, and I couldn't even remember the last time I had eaten some; it took a great deal of the finest white rice to make *duk*. I had nibbled the slices of *duk* slowly, slowly, to make them last as long as possible, and Jung-shin had seemed very pleased at my appreciation.

Now it was my turn to treat her. I went to the kitchen shelves and asked Omoni for some popping corn. There wasn't much left in the little bag. I took nearly all of it and put it in a hollow gourd. Then I fetched two pennies from my savings box and put them in my coin purse. I also brought along an empty grain sack.

On fine days the popcorn man roamed the streets of our town, wheeling a little cart. He sold corn, or for two cents he would pop the corn you brought him.

We found him a few blocks away and gave him the gourd of corn. The popping was always fun to watch. He poured the dried kernels into one end of a device that looked rather

43

like a pot-bellied cannon, which contained some kind of heating element. After a few minutes, popped corn came shooting out of the cannon's barrel and was caught in a wire mesh basket. When the popping sound stopped, the popcorn man took the basket off while I held my sack underneath so the fluffy popcorn could fall into it.

Jung-shin and I walked along the street munching our snack. We turned the corner, and I said, "My uncle's shop is on this street. Why don't we go there?"

This was really what I had had in mind all along. If I showed Jung-shin around the shop, I might learn something about what Uncle was doing.

Jung-shin agreed eagerly. She had often heard me speak of Uncle but had never met him.

When we reached the shop, Uncle greeted me with his usual cheerful smile. In return I said, "Uncle, I would like you to meet a friend of mine. This is Pak Jung-shin."

Jung-shin bowed politely to Uncle, and he smiled at her. I was proud to be introducing my friend; she looked so pretty, with a new white collar on her uniform.

"I am pleased to meet you," Uncle said. "Tell me about your family."

"My father is Pak Sung-joon," Jung-shin replied. "My family moved here a few months ago. My father has a new job at the bank."

Uncle nodded, but the look in his eyes changed. The little lines around his eyes that made his smile so pleasant seemed to disappear. His eyes suddenly looked almost blank, expressionless, even though his mouth was still smiling.

Or was I only imagining things?

Then Uncle turned to me. "I'm sorry, Sun-hee, but I am

busy just now. You and your friend must stop by another time. Perhaps then I will be able to print something special for her."

Jung-shin was delighted by his offer and thanked him politely, but I was puzzled. It was quiet in the shop—there were no customers, and Uncle was not running between the printing press and the counter and the paper storeroom. But of course I honored his request, and we turned to leave.

Uncle walked us to the door—and this, too, puzzled me. He waved to us as we walked away. I took one last glance over my shoulder and saw Uncle scanning the street carefully.

I didn't know what to think.

When I got home, I took my shoes off as usual, put on my straw slippers, and went to find Tae-yul in the workshop area behind the house.

"I went to see Uncle just now," I said. Then I hesitated. I'd intended to tell him about Uncle's behavior with Jung-shin, and how he'd looked up and down the street after we left. But now it seemed silly. I didn't want Tae-yul to think I was making a big deal out of nothing.

I bit my lip, then said, "I didn't discover anything."

He sighed. "I haven't been able to find out anything either. We'll just have to keep trying. Now, don't forget—whatever you find out, don't do anything about it. Come and tell me first. We're working on this together, remember?"

I nodded automatically, but I felt annoyed. He still thought I was a baby.

How I wished I could simply talk to Uncle about it. But I knew this would be unfair. Asking him to talk to us about things Abuji disapproved of would be disrespectful.

The weeks passed without either of us learning anything more about Uncle's activities. The mystery even slipped my mind sometimes, because I had other things to think about. I would soon graduate from elementary school; in the New Year I'd start junior high school. I had passed all my examinations with good marks. But I didn't stop studying; I wanted to be ready for the more difficult junior high courses.

One wintry afternoon I was in the sitting room, bent over my books, when suddenly I heard shouting in the lane. It was Tae-yul's voice, but I couldn't make out what he was saying. I rushed to the door.

"The Japanese have attacked America!" he shouted breathlessly as he rushed inside. He tore off his cap as he came in, his cheeks red with cold and excitement.

Abuji and Omoni, too, had come to the courtyard—Abuji from his room, Omoni from the kitchen. "Tae-yul, calm yourself," Abuji said. "What are you saying?"

"It was on the radio—everyone's talking about it—"

Abuji frowned. "Possibly a rumor. It seems highly unlikely—"

Tae-yul crossed the courtyard to the sitting room and turned on the radio. The transmission was static-riddled and somewhat garbled, but we could still make out some words: "... *spectacular victory* ... *Pearl Harbor* ... *Hawaii* ... *important military base* ... *enemy completely taken by surprise* ... *heavy damage* ..." While Abuji and Tae-yul crouched by the radio, I stood to one side and whispered translations to Omoni.

After several minutes Abuji turned off the radio, his face grave.

"It is a very serious action," he said to Tae-yul. "It means Japan is at war with the United States. I fear hard times ahead."

Just then Uncle rushed in, as excited as Tae-yul had been. He was waving a flyer in one hand. "You've all heard, have you? It's incredible news! Tae-yul, I need your help at the shop. The Military Command has ordered hundreds of these flyers to be printed and distributed all over town—"

Abuji held up his hand. "Surely, Tae-yul, you have studying to do."

Tae-yul looked from Uncle to Abuji and back again. I could tell that he wanted to go with Uncle, to be part of the excitement.

Uncle bowed his head. "Hyungnim, I will secure permission for Tae-yul to miss school tomorrow, and to make up his lessons at a later date. This is very important work. Everyone must know the details of this event. His help is sorely needed."

Abuji pursed his lips for a moment, then finally nodded at Tae-yul. "See that you work twice as hard on your studies tonight," he said.

Tae-yul bowed hastily. "Yes, Abuji. Thank you, Abuji." He jammed his cap back on and hurried out the door with Uncle.

A quick flame of anger flared in me. I'd have liked to have gone with Uncle as well. I could've helped stack the flyers and bind them with twine while Tae-yul delivered them. Why should he have all the fun?

I wandered out into the lane. My steps took me in the direction of Tomo's house. These days Tomo and I played together less often than we used to. We weren't angry with each other or anything like that; it was just that we'd outgrown our childhood games, and I was spending more

47

time with Jung-shin. But Tomo and I still sometimes thought of each other when we had time to play.

He was in the yard when I arrived, but so were three other boys I didn't know. When I saw them, I pretended I was only passing by, but Tomo caught sight of me and ran out to the lane.

"Keoko, look! See what my father brought me." He displayed his new toy, a beautiful model airplane made of wood and sturdy paper. "It's a Flying Dragon, exactly like the ones flown by the Imperial pilots."

He ran in a circle holding the plane over his head. "*Ack-ack-ack-ack-ack!*" he shouted. "The Dragon swoops over Pearl Harbor—he finds a target—he fires! It's a direct hit! The enemy plane crashes—smoke and flames everywhere! The nimble Dragon escapes!"

I felt a little bashful with those other boys around, but I did want to look at the plane. "Can I see it again, Tomo?" I asked.

He came to a stop before me and held the plane out. "You can hold it," he said generously.

"Hey!" one of the boys protested. "You wouldn't let any of us even touch it."

Tomo looked at him with disdain. "You might be too rough with it. Keoko will be careful."

I was pleased that he trusted me, but his words also made me anxious. I held the plane for only a few moments, admiring the glossy paper of its wings and the propellers that really spun. Then I gave it back to him, thinking how much Tae-yul would like to have a plane like this one. He loved mechanical things.

"The Imperial forces have huge fleets of these planes,"

Tomo said excitedly. "The Americans don't stand a chance! *Ack-ack-ack-ack-ack*—" and he began running around again with his plane held high.

"Kill them! Kill the Americans!" another boy shouted.

"Kill the Americans!" The others took up the chant. "Kill the Americans, kill the Americans!"

"All of them!" shouted the first boy.

"Even the babies?" I said. The words slipped out before I could stop them. The boys stopped chanting and stared at me.

Tomo slowed down and zoomed his plane over to me. "Keoko, don't you remember the movie?" he said.

We'd been shown a short film in our classrooms a few weeks earlier. Onishi-san had gone from room to room with the movie projector until all the students had seen the film. None of us had ever seen a movie before.

The teacher helped Onishi-san hang a sheet on the wall, then instructed me, as Class Leader, to choose a few girls to help me cover the windows with heavy pieces of paper. The classroom looked different darkened like that, almost scary.

Then Onishi-san turned on the projector, and suddenly there was a picture on the sheet! A picture so bright it almost blinded me. When my eyes stopped hurting a few seconds later, I saw that the people in the picture were moving. You could even tell when they were talking, their lips moving quickly. They looked so real it was hard to believe that if I'd touched them I would only have been touching cloth.

Everyone gasped and murmured in surprise. Then Onishi-san started talking. The film, he said, was to teach us what Americans were like.

The pictures were of white people, usually riding horses and wearing big white hats, shooting and killing other people. Onishi-san told us that the Americans hated all people with black hair and killed even the women and babies of their enemies just to amuse themselves.

At the time I barely heard him. It hadn't mattered what the movie was about; the moving pictures themselves were what fascinated me. The rest of that day, and for days afterward, those flickering images kept returning to my mind, almost like a dream.

Now Onishi-san's words came back to me. It was true that all the people being shot at in the film had long black hair. But I'd heard Uncle and Abuji talk about America. I hadn't understood everything they said, but I knew that America was a very large country. There were things about it that they both admired. Education, I remembered Abuji saying, and Uncle talking about freedom.

I couldn't believe that Abuji and Uncle would admire people who killed babies for fun.

The boys were still staring at me; I felt my face growing red. "The movie," I mumbled, just to say something, anything.

"Yes," one of the other boys said. "If the Americans have the chance, they'll kill all of us. Because we have black hair. We have to kill them first!"

Tomo glanced at me quickly, then at his friends. "Yes, but we won't need to kill any babies," he said. "We'll kill all their soldiers—bomb their cities—they'll surrender like dogs!" And he zoomed his plane over their heads. "*Ack-ack-ack-ack-ack!*"

Tomo ran up the lane, with his friends following him. I waited for a moment, hoping he'd look back at me, but he kept going. I turned the other way and walked home, feeling confused and a little sad.

I was glad that Tomo didn't want to kill babies. Still, he and his friends all seemed to think that playing at killing was fun. Was it because they were boys?

Even the talk about killing had made my stomach feel cold.

10. Tae-yul (1942)

A few weeks after the news about Pearl Harbor, I'm riding my bike home from Uncle's shop.

I hear a humming noise—faint at first, but then stronger.

Like a car. But not a car. Some sort of engine.

I look up and down the street. Nothing. Just people walking.

The noise comes even closer, and it's not coming from the street.

It's coming from the sky.

I look up—and there it is. An airplane!

It flies straight over the town—right above me! I duck my head and immediately fall off my bike.

Afterward, I feel like a complete idiot—the plane wasn't anywhere close to my head. But everyone else on the street was looking up at the sky, too. So I don't think anyone saw me fall.

I watch the plane until it flies out of sight to the west, then pick up my bike. But I don't start riding again right away—I walk, pushing the bicycle beside me.

I've seen pictures of airplanes, and Uncle told me about seeing one a long time ago, when I was only a baby. But I never thought I'd see one myself.

I walk along, trying to remember every little thing about it. The noise—how it was so small at first, like a fly buzzing. Then louder, louder, so loud you couldn't hear yourself think. And then fading . . . like the sound had a shape, almost. Small at the ends and huge in the middle.

The way the plane looked—like a cross when it was just overhead, but a tiny black dot in the distance.

And the speed! What would it feel like to travel so fast and so high?

I jump on my bike and start pedaling. Faster, faster, like if I get it going fast enough, it'll lift right off the ground. My ears are aching, my eyes tearing from the cold wind, but I hardly notice. I coast, take my hands off the handlebars, and hold them up over my head.

"AI-EEEEEE!" I shout, not caring if anyone hears me.

Is this what it feels like to fly?

Radio Tokyo. It used to be always the same old stuff: the brave Japanese army in Manchuria, the great deeds and sayings of the Emperor.

But now things are different. Now the announcer is always excited. News of the war all day long: Hong Kong. Singapore. Burma. The Philippines. The Japanese are advancing so quickly. In just six months, south to New Guinea, near Australia, and east to Attu, near Alaska.

The names of these strange places become part of our lessons every day. Teacher sticks Japanese flag-pins on the conquered countries. Nothing can stop them—soon the whole world will be full of little Japanese flags. . . .

So much good news—for the Japanese. Around town you can tell. Uncle's business is booming. I get to help print signs for the merchants to hang in their windows. *Victory! Strength to the Japanese army!* Things like that. The signs make the streets look like a celebration, all the time. Everybody is more cheerful and even the guards aren't as cruel.

It's so odd. The war is going well for the Japanese—which makes life better for Koreans too. If the Japanese win the war, will things be better still?

Planes fly over town a lot now, on their way from Japan to Manchuria. Every week a plane or two or even a whole formation.

I hate it when they come while I'm in school. Then I hear them but can't see them. It nearly drives me crazy.

I think about planes all the time, trying to imagine what it would be like to fly in one. I can feel the hum of the plane beneath me as I start the engine. Like my bicycle, only much noisier, grander.

But I can't imagine actually taking off. It wouldn't be like jumping off the ground—you'd be sitting up in the cockpit.

And then, in the air, looking down on everything. I've gone mountain climbing a few times. Hard work, but fun to reach the top. The whole world spread out below you, everything so small. That must be what things look like from a plane.

But on the mountain you're standing still. In a plane you'd be moving. Sitting, but moving. Flying! It has to be the most amazing feeling in the world.

11. Sun-hee

After the attack on Pearl Harbor, things seemed to change very quickly. More Japanese soldiers appeared in the streets, and the government immediately made dozens of new laws.

53

One of them was the law about neighborhood associations.

The Japanese wanted us to gather quickly in case there was ever a war emergency. They organized the associations to teach us how to do this. In each neighborhood one person was named the block leader. The Japanese officials would give information to the block leader, who used a megaphone to call everyone from their homes. We had to drop whatever we were doing and hurry out into the street.

Everyone stood in line. The block leader pointed to the first family, and the head of the household—usually the father— called out, "One!" at the top of his lungs. Then, "Two!" from the next family, and so on down the line until the leader had heard the number "Ten." There were ten households in every association. Then the leader would make whatever announcements the Japanese wanted him to make over the megaphone.

One of our neighbors was an old woman named Mrs. Ahn. She had had a very unfortunate life. Her husband had divorced her, and she'd returned home to live with her parents. They had died within a few years of each other. Now she was all alone in the world.

She was the only divorced person I'd ever met. People in the neighborhood avoided her; they said she was bad luck. I didn't think that was true—she seemed pretty much like everybody else. All the same, I didn't like visiting her house; it always seemed empty and forlorn, as if the air inside were never warmed by laughter.

Omoni felt sorry for Mrs. Ahn, and we usually stopped by her house on our way to the market to ask if she needed anything. And whenever there was a call over the megaphone for a neighborhood association meeting, Omoni rushed out the door to help her.

54

At the very first accounting, we didn't know what to do. The leader had to shout over and over to get us to form a line by household. It was only Omoni and me at home that day; the men were all somewhere else.

Soldiers walked up and down the street pounding on doors and making sure that everyone was out of their houses. Then they watched sternly as we tried to obey the leader's instructions. Sometimes they shouted orders or prodded people with their sticks to make them stand in a straighter line.

The leader told us to count off by household. The count began and progressed quickly down the line.

"*Ichi!*"

"*Ni!*"

"*San!*"

"*Shi!*"

"*Go!*"

It was Mrs. Ahn's turn; she was sixth in line, and as the only member of her household, she had to shout the number herself. We were standing right next to her, and she looked at us in a terrible panic.

All at once I realized what was wrong.

Mrs. Ahn couldn't speak Japanese. She didn't know how to say "six" in Japanese.

The rhythm of the count was broken. The silence seemed to last forever. I tried to help her. "*Roku,*" I whispered. But I didn't raise my voice—I was afraid of the soldiers. And she didn't hear me.

Finally, she yelled, "*Yo-sut!*" I gasped in horror; beside me I felt Omoni stiffen. The whole line of people seemed to ripple in surprise.

Yo-sut was the word for six—*in Korean.*

At once a soldier strode forward and pulled her out of the line. "What did you say, old woman?"

Mrs. Ahn fell to her knees. I knew she couldn't understand the soldier's words, but the anger in his voice was unmistakable. "I am sorry, honorable sir—I did not know—"

Her speaking Korean made the soldier even angrier. "Stupid cow!" he yelled. "What kind of dung is your brain made of? Japanese has been the official language of this country for thirty years now! How could you not know?"

And then he hit her with his stick on her head and shoulders. I was standing so close I could hear the *thunk* of the wood as it met her flesh, and the sharper crack against her skull. She fell over and lay senseless.

"*Roku*, you stupid cow! *Roku*," he taunted her limp body. Then he looked at Omoni. "Continue!"

Omoni drew a quick breath and shouted, "*Shichi!*" Then she stepped out of line to help Mrs. Ahn, who was already regaining her senses. It seemed that the blows hadn't actually knocked her out; she'd simply fainted from fear and pain. But she was bruised and dazed and needed help.

As Omoni knelt in the street, the soldier turned toward us. "You there! What are you doing?"

Omoni bowed her head and spoke in a meek voice. "I am sure the honorable sir is a man who respects his elders. Mrs. Ahn is senior to me, and it is my duty to assist her."

I was paralyzed with fear. Omoni's voice seemed timid, but her words were like iron. I'd never heard her speak like that to a man before. How could she speak to a soldier in this way? Would he beat her, too?

The soldier's mouth and eyes narrowed as he looked at her for a moment. Then he made a dismissive gesture with his hand. "Get her out of the way," he snarled.

Omoni and I took Mrs. Ahn to her home. I made tea while Omoni took care of her wounds. My hands shook so much that I spilled tea all over the table. But when Omoni saw the mess I'd made, she didn't scold me. She put her hand on my shoulder and pressed down gently, as if she were trying to stop my trembling. It worked. I reached up and touched her hand and felt a little better.

After a few days, when Mrs. Ahn was fully recovered, Omoni sent me to her house to teach her to count in Japanese. I went without complaining because I felt guilty that I hadn't helped her in the line. If I'd been braver—if I'd said "*roku*" loud enough for her to hear—maybe she wouldn't have been beaten.

When I arrived, she invited me in. I sat on the floor and she served tea. I sipped at mine silently. After a few minutes she put down her cup and looked at me. "You will teach me to count," she said.

"Yes, Ajima."

"Good. Let us begin."

I said the words as I held up the correct number of fingers; this was how the teacher had taught the class when I first started school. I'd already been able to count in Japanese because of my friendship with Tomo. "*Ichi–ni–san–shi–go*," I said. I paused there, and Mrs. Ahn echoed the words slowly.

Then I went on: "*Roku–shichi—*"

She shook her head and stopped me. "No," she said. "To five, again."

It seemed she'd rather learn the first five very well before going on. Maybe that was a good idea. "*Ichi–ni–san–shi–go*," I said again.

We did this a few more times, then Mrs. Ahn said the

57

numbers by herself. After she'd done it three times in a row without a mistake, she sat back.

"That will do," she said, and smiled. "You are a good teacher. Tell your mother I said that you needn't come back anymore."

I bowed my head, puzzled. I didn't want to contradict her, yet I felt I had to say something. "But, Ajima, you have only learned to count to five. Surely we should continue, to ten—" There were ten households in our association; she would need to be able to count at least that high.

"No." Mrs. Ahn's voice rang out strongly. I looked at her, surprised. "No," she said again. She lowered her voice a little. "I will tell you why. I have nothing in this world—you know that. Everyone knows that. No children, no family. Alone here all day with nothing but my thoughts."

Her voice was still fierce as she continued, "They cannot have my thoughts. I will not allow it."

She held up her hand. "*Ichi–ni–san–shi–go*," she said, finger by finger. "One hand. Five fingers of thought—that is all I will give them. Not one finger more."

I rose to leave. At the door I turned and bowed deeply to Mrs. Ahn. She seemed surprised and pleased by this and nodded at me kindly.

At home I told Omoni what had happened at Mrs. Ahn's house. She said nothing for a few moments. Then she looked at me steadily and put her hands on my shoulders. "Sun-hee, it will be our job, yours and mine, to fetch Mrs. Ahn quickly whenever there is a neighborhood accounting," she said. "As soon as you hear the megaphone, one of us must be out the door, quick as a cat. If I am delayed, you must go yourself. Is this clear?"

58

I frowned. Mrs. Ahn was elderly, but she could still get around quite well by herself. . . .

"Sun-hee, do you understand? One of us must go quickly—every time—"

And suddenly I did understand. I looked at Omoni and nodded. She gripped my shoulders firmly, then gave me a hug.

Yes, we'd have to be quick—to make sure that Mrs. Ahn would always be one of the first five households in line.

12. Tae-yul (1942-43)

The neighborhood accountings are such a nuisance. We have to stop whatever we're doing, go out, and stand around on the street. It's always at least half an hour before we're dismissed.

Once I stayed in the house when I heard the megaphone. It should've been all right—Omoni and Sun-hee were there. But when Sun-hee came back, she told me Omoni had been very nervous, looking over her shoulder and wondering if I was going to show up. If the Japanese found out I hadn't come to the accounting, Omoni might get in trouble. Maybe Abuji, too. So now I always go.

One morning Teacher is excited. "Class!" he says. "The Emperor has sent a gift to every student in the land. In honor of the victories of His Imperial forces in the rubber-producing countries of the Tropics, you are each to receive a rubber ball!" And he pulls a big crate of balls from behind his desk.

The balls are the size of an apple. They're a dirty yellow color, and stamped with the words "May the Emperor Reign for Ten Thousand Years in Malaya, Burma, Singapore!"

Every student gets one. Then Teacher announces that there won't be any classes that day. Instead, we're to bow at the shrine to thank the Emperor. After that we're free to play with our new balls.

We run around the schoolyard, yelling our heads off. The balls are perfect for a game of catch. Or for bouncing—they soar right over your head if you throw them down hard enough. But they're no good for soccer—too small, and they skip over your foot if you try to make a pass.

The military attaché raises the megaphone and shouts into it. We all freeze where we are. I've just thrown my ball against the wall. I stand still and listen, but watch my ball to make sure I can find it after the announcement.

"We are glad to see the students enjoying their gifts!" the military attaché says. "The Emperor's generosity knows no bounds. We expect all of you to express your gratitude by working ever harder at your studies, to become good citizens of the Empire. Long live His Divine Majesty!"

"Long live His Divine Majesty!" we echo. Like we always do. A short silence, then everyone goes back to playing.

Except me. I walk over to where my ball has rolled into a corner, pick it up, and put it into my backpack.

"Hey, Nobuo!" my friend Sung-kwon shouts. Sung-kwon is his real name; in school he's Osamu. "Aren't you going to play some more?"

"Nah, I'm going home now. See you tomorrow." I walk toward the gate, to my bicycle.

Maybe I should stay. Especially to play with Sung-kwon. He's feeling low these days. His older brother, Sung-ho, a college student, was forced to enlist in the Japanese army. I went with Sung-kwon to the train station to see him off. Sung-kwon has been in a bad mood ever since.

But I don't feel like playing anymore—all because of that stupid announcement. "Express your gratitude," they'd said.

What they take: our rice, our language, our names. What they give: little rubber balls.

I can't feel grateful about such a bad deal.

There are more and more neighborhood accountings. They're always the same. First, praise for the Imperial Army's victories. Everyone has to clap and cheer. And then we're asked to help in the war effort.

Asked to help—another lie. What it means is, the army takes away our things.

First our radios. That makes Uncle really mad. Not that it matters as far as getting the news, he says—we have only Radio Tokyo anyway. But it's the principle of it, them taking whatever they want.

Abuji says it's no use getting angry.

But how can he not get angry?

The weather gets colder. They take our blankets and warm clothing. The wind cuts through my jacket as I ride down the street. The jacket's too small—the sleeves barely reach my wrists. And it hikes up my back when I lean over the handlebars. Omoni and Sun-hee are taking apart old clothes, remaking them. But so far no luck with a new jacket for me.

Being cold is sometimes all right. It makes me pedal even faster. I swoop around the corner of our street, *whoosh*, so smooth. . . . I always get the timing right. Turning the handlebars at the exact moment, just enough so I don't lose speed.

A shout. "You there! On the bicycle! Halt, in the name of His Imperial Majesty!"

I skid to a stop and turn the bike partway around. Two

soldiers are standing near the gate to our house. I get off, walk the bike toward them.

One soldier throws his cigarette down, jerks his chin at my bicycle. "What's that you're riding?" he asks. "You call that a bicycle?"

He walks around it, pokes at it. "Look at those handlebars. Does water run through them? And what kind of seat is that? Man, you must have one sore butt."

It makes me so mad, him insulting my bike like that. But there's nothing I can do about it, of course. I just stand there with my head down, hoping he'll get tired of teasing me and let me go home.

His friend shoves him a little. "Get out of the way and let me look at this thing," he says. "You know, it's really not so bad—you saw him come around the corner. It has pretty good speed."

His voice is a lot friendlier than the first soldier's. But his words scare me. If he likes my bicycle . . .

Just then Abuji comes out of the house and walks down the path toward us. He nods at the soldiers. "Good afternoon, gentlemen. Is there a problem?"

The soldiers straighten up quickly and stand side by side. The second soldier glances briefly at his friend. "No problem, Sensei."

He calls Abuji "Sensei"—teacher. I let out my breath silently, relieved.

"No problem," the soldier repeats. "We are commandeering this bicycle in the name of His Imperial Majesty. I am sure Sensei appreciates that with the war on, the Imperial forces require every available mode of transportation to further the Emperor's glorious cause. The Emperor is most grateful to the citizens of his realm for their willingness to make sacrifices on behalf of the military."

My hands freeze. I grip the bike, one hand on the seat, the other on the frame. The soldier steps forward and tries to take the bike from me. But I don't let go. We tug it back and forth between us.

Finally, I shout, "No! It's mine! You can't take it away!"

Abuji is so quick. He pries my hands open and pulls me back toward him. "I apologize for my son's disrespectful behavior," he says, bowing his head.

I can't move or speak. I can only watch as they walk a little way up the street, the bicycle between them. Then one of them—the second soldier—jumps on and begins pedaling. He laughs at his friend over his shoulder. His friend makes some sort of joke back.

They've already forgotten me. Treated me like I'm some sort of dog, with a bone they can take away anytime they feel like it.

I wrench myself away from Abuji and whirl around to face him. For a second I feel like shouting. I swallow once, hard. Then I say, low, "You just let them take it. You didn't even try to stop them. Couldn't you have thought of something—anything—"

Abuji's face goes pale but he doesn't say anything. I know what he's thinking. Even though I'm not shouting, I'm questioning his decision. It's the rudest thing a son can do. I'm almost scared myself—I've never spoken to him that way before, I can hardly believe those words came out of my mouth.

But then I think of my bike again. Of all the work Uncle and I did. And Abuji's silence makes me crazy. "He called you

'Sensei'! He knew you're the vice-principal—he might've listened to you. At least you could have tried!"

Abuji only shakes his head. Then, "I am sorry about your bicycle, Tae-yul." He turns and goes into the house.

I stand there, staring at his back. I'm so mad my stomach feels sick.

Sorry? He isn't sorry. He doesn't care at all.

13. Sun-hee

I knew something was wrong. All evening Tae-yul's face was like a rock, cold and hard and gray. Later I saw him and Uncle talking in the garden; I watched as Uncle shook his head and put his arm around Tae-yul's shoulder. I could tell that Uncle was trying to comfort him. But, of course, nobody told me anything.

In the morning I left the house and walked along, waiting for the moment when Tae-yul would zoom by me on his bicycle, as he always did. I was nearly halfway to school when I finally turned around, wondering where he was—he usually passed me long before this point. And I saw him a few blocks behind me, walking.

The bicycle could have been broken, but I knew at once this wasn't what had happened. I remembered his face from the night before. His bike had broken lots of times. He'd never looked as sad as he did now.

And he went on looking like that for days afterward. No, not sad—that isn't quite right. Sad and angry, mixed up together. Angry at Abuji, for some reason. Tae-yul seemed to stiffen whenever Abuji came into the room. If Abuji spoke to him, he answered with a grunt or mumbled something. I could hardly believe Tae-yul was being so disrespectful. Whenever they were in a room together, things were really uncomfortable—like a blanket of bad feeling over us all.

As if this weren't enough, life at home seemed even grayer and sadder because Uncle wasn't around as much. He was working longer and longer hours at his shop. There were nights when he didn't come home at all. Omoni worried about his health; she feared he wasn't eating or sleeping enough.

Sometimes she sent me or Tae-yul with some supper for Uncle. More and more often when I reached the shop, I'd find the door closed. I'd call out as I pushed open the door, and Uncle would come hurrying out of the back room. He always greeted me cheerfully and made a joke about how I'd saved his life by bringing food. And then he would walk me out and look up and down the street before he closed the door behind me.

I was curious about the way he scanned the street; he'd done the same when I came by with Jung-shin. Time after time I almost said something to Tae-yul. But he had to have seen it, too, and he hadn't said anything.

One evening in early summer Omoni sent me out with Uncle's supper. As I left our house, I saw a movement out of the corner of my eye that startled me. Someone was standing in the long shadow of the wall of the house next door.

It was Tomo.

"Tomo! What are you doing hiding there—you nearly frightened me to death!"

"Hello," he said. But he didn't step out of the shadow. He leaned forward a little and looked quickly up and down the lane. Then he jerked his head, beckoning me to join him.

I was pleased to see him, but the way he was acting made me look around nervously as I walked toward him. We were at different schools now, so it had been a while since we'd last met. I noticed how much he had grown. We'd always been close to the same height, but now he was nearly a head taller than me.

"I was just passing," he said carefully, "and I thought I'd stop by and see if you were around. I've been . . . thinking about something." His eyes flickered to my face, then down to the ground.

He was definitely uncomfortable. "Thinking about what?" I asked as gently as I could.

Aimlessly, he kicked a stone at his feet. Then he squatted down on his haunches and picked it up. He examined it carefully for a moment, as if it might hold a secret. Suddenly, his face seemed to brighten; he stood up again and held the stone out to me. "Do you remember when we used to collect stones like this? To build our cities?"

I smiled. "Of course I remember. We built lots of cities—some really good ones. Remember the stadium?"

"Yes . . . I've been thinking about those days," Tomo said, still speaking slowly. "About the little things your uncle made for us. Do you know what happened to them?"

Uncle had often stopped by to admire the cities. Once he gave me a present: several tiny signs with real printing on them. He'd made them at his shop. They said things like GROCERY STORE and RAILWAY STATION. I was so proud when I brought them to show Tomo. They made our city look much more real.

Another time Uncle made a lot of little things out of wire. Lampposts and gates for outside the houses, tables for inside, even a tiny wire bicycle. We were delighted.

66

Now I frowned. "What happened to what? The little signs? Or the wire things? I suppose they all got lost. I'm not sure. But I know I don't have them at home anymore."

"Hmm," he said. "I wish I knew. . . . It's too bad—he made some really nice things."

An odd feeling was growing inside me—in my throat, in my stomach, at the back of my neck. The way Tomo was looking at me, talking so seriously about a few silly, childish toys—it was as if he were saying one thing while thinking another.

He took a step toward the lane. "I have to go now. I just wanted to say, I always thought it was a shame . . . that we didn't keep those things safe somehow. It was so nice of your uncle—I thought of it especially today. . . ."

His voice trailed off. He glanced up and down the lane again, then looked at me one last time as if he were about to say something more. Instead, he handed me the stone, touched his cap, and hurried away.

I stood still for a moment. *Saying one thing but thinking another*—I sensed that Tomo had wanted to tell me something that he couldn't say openly. I looked at the stone he'd given me. The houses and shops we'd built, out of stones like this one, the little things inside them that Uncle had made for us . . . Uncle. He'd mentioned Uncle a couple of times. . . .

A shame . . . your uncle . . . not safe . . . especially today . . .

I raised my head in a moment of stunned realization.

Tomo had brought me a warning.

Something bad was going to happen.

To Uncle.

I dropped the lunch box that held Uncle's dinner and began to run.

———

The few blocks to Uncle's shop had never seemed so long. I couldn't go as fast as I wanted to—I had to keep an eye out for military guards who would surely question me if they saw me running in a panic. I stayed close to the buildings, hurrying along and pausing before I turned a corner.

I thought perhaps I should go home first, to talk to Tae-yul. But my heart was pounding, my thoughts were pounding, and I couldn't seem to stop my feet. As I neared the center of town where there were more guards, I slowed down and tried to walk casually. Thinking, thinking the whole time.

If I went home and told Tae-yul, what would he do? He'd go warn Uncle, surely. He might even be angry at me for wasting time. *I thought of it especially today,* Tomo had said. Whatever it was, it might happen any minute now. The sooner the better, to tell Uncle. This must be what Abuji had been afraid of, what he'd tried to warn Uncle about.

Or else Tae-yul might say it was nothing, that we should wait and see. That I'd imagined everything—that Tomo had just been chatting about nothing. Tae-yul might think I was silly for getting so excited.

But he hadn't been there. He hadn't seen Tomo's uneasy face or heard the worry in his voice.

I *knew* I was right. I knew Tomo. He was telling me more than he'd said. I could feel it.

I quickened my steps again. Now I could see the shop. The door was closed. I ran the last half block and pushed the door open.

There was no one in the shop itself, but I heard low voices coming from the back room. "Uncle?" I called shakily.

Uncle came out with the usual cheerful expression on his

face, though I could see from the dark smudges under his eyes that he was very tired.

"Sun-hee!" he said. "Where's my supper? Did you eat it on the way here?"

I was too frightened to respond to his little joke. "Uncle—please, you must leave here—quickly—something bad—I don't know when—"

The light in Uncle's eyes faded at once. He came toward me and put his arm around me. "Sun-hee, calm yourself. What's the matter?"

I took a deep breath, swallowed hard, and began again. "Uncle, Tomo came to see me just now. He said—he said something bad is going to happen. To you. He didn't say exactly when or what it was, but—but he was very worried, I could tell. And it will be soon. Uncle, please, what is it? What was Tomo talking about?"

Uncle didn't look surprised. He didn't even question me. "Wait here," he said, and went to the back room. He spoke to someone; I could hear another voice answer him, but couldn't make out the words. Then there was a sudden flurry of activity—the sound of papers being rustled. I heard the front door rattle from the draft as the other person left by the back door.

Uncle returned and came out from behind the counter. He pulled me close to him and gave me a quick hug. "I am not going home tonight, Sun-hee. I won't be home again for a long time. How long, I'm not sure. I can't answer your questions right now—you must hurry home." He paused for a moment. "Tell Tae-yul I said he can tell you what he knows."

Something bad *was* about to happen. Uncle had been expecting it. Not from me, maybe, not in this way, but he was ready. *He* knew what was happening, even if I didn't. And he had a plan, somewhere to go.

A tiny voice in my head said, *You were right! Aren't you glad you didn't go to Tae-yul first?* But it was silenced almost immediately by other voices—cries of fear for Uncle's safety.

He reached out and gave my hair a gentle tug. "Now go. And continue to be brave, Sun-hee. You have been very brave tonight—I am proud of you."

And he walked me to the door.

I stood in the street for a moment. The sun was sinking behind the hills that surrounded the town. Its last rays seemed to be a blur of gold. I blinked to clear my vision, and a tear rolled down my cheek. Hastily, I wiped it away and set off toward home.

When I reached the lane, I caught sight of the lunch box I'd dropped. It made me feel bad. Whatever Uncle was doing—wherever he was going—he surely would have liked a bite to eat. As I bent over to pick it up, I saw the stone Tomo had given me, and I picked that up, too.

I stepped into the corridor that led to our inner courtyard.

14. *Tae-yul*

Sun-hee comes into the house with Uncle's lunch box in her hand. I'm in the sitting room with Abuji, Omoni's in the courtyard covering the *kimchee* jar—we all see her come in.

Sun-hee looks at Abuji. "Uncle says . . . he won't be coming home tonight." Her voice is shaky, like she might start crying any second. "He'll be . . . away for a while. He doesn't know how long."

Abuji closes his eyes. He doesn't say anything at first, then speaks without opening them. "If anyone should ask, we will tell the truth. We do not know where my brother has gone, or when he will be back. We do not know. That is all any of you need to say."

He opens his eyes and looks at us hard. "And whatever happens tonight, you are not to leave the house."

When he says those last words, he's looking right at *me*.

He doesn't seem surprised. Upset, maybe, but not surprised. The same for Omoni. They don't ask Sun-hee even a single question. It's almost like they expected this. *Whatever happens tonight* . . . what's going to happen?

Sun-hee looks scared. She catches my eye and slips out the back door. I follow her a few minutes later.

She's crouching in the middle of the vegetable garden pulling weeds. The sun is almost gone, but there's still enough light to see.

We work for a few minutes side by side. I know she's dying to ask questions. But she waits a little while before saying, "Uncle said you're to tell me what you know."

"I don't know everything," I say. "And what I do know, I found out only yesterday. I wasn't keeping it a secret from you, honest—I just hadn't found the right time to tell you."

It's the truth. She looks doubtful, but nods for me to continue.

"Uncle works for the resistance," I tell her. "For the illegal independence movement. He's been working with them for a while now. At night, or when no one's around, he prints a resistance newspaper.

"That's why he's forcing himself to be on good terms with

all his Japanese customers. To make them think he's *chin-il-pa*, so they won't suspect him."

The relief I felt when I learned this yesterday! Uncle isn't *chin-il-pa!* He's only pretending to be—so well that he even fooled me. I should have known better. I should never have doubted him.

Sun-hee is so quiet I wonder if she's heard me. I look over at her. Her face is gray in the dim light. Finally, she whispers, "What else do you know?"

I tell her that Uncle said the police were hanging around the shop. A lot. For no reason. He thought they suspected him and that something might happen.

But so soon? I don't think he thought it would be so soon.

My turn to ask questions. "Did he say where he was going?"

She shakes her head.

"Into hiding," I say, thinking hard. "It's a big movement— he must have friends who'll help him. But how did he find out? I mean, how did he know he should escape tonight?"

Sun-hee says, "I told him."

I look at her, my mouth open. I can't believe it—*she* told him? How did she know? She speaks again quickly. "I mean, not because I knew—I didn't know anything. But Tomo came to see me tonight. He told me."

I whistle between my teeth. "Tomo! I never would have guessed."

"Opah, do our parents know about all this?"

I hesitate.

She pushes out her lips. "Uncle said you could tell me. *Everything.*"

"All right," I say. "Our parents know that Uncle works for the resistance. But that's all—Uncle doesn't want them to know anything more than that. And I think that suits Abuji

72

just fine—he prefers it that way." I can feel my throat tightening a little, but I keep talking. "Abuji also told Uncle to leave me out of it. But Uncle told me anyway because—because he said it was important for me to know."

Sun-hee gasps. I know what she's thinking: Uncle going against Abuji's wishes? "Sun-hee, I don't mean to be disrespectful to Abuji." My words come slowly. "But it's like he's blind to what's happening here. He goes to work, he comes home and buries himself in his books—he doesn't care about what the Japanese are doing to us. As long as he can study his books, that's all that matters to him."

Now she looks almost ill, hearing me talk about Abuji like that. She whispers, "Opah, surely Abuji's only trying to protect Uncle. That's his job—to keep us all safe."

I stand, take a few steps away from her, and clench and unclench my fists. It's so hard to say what's in my head. I turn back toward her. "What Uncle and others like him are doing—it's more important than anything. We aren't Japanese—we're Korean. But we'll never be allowed to truly *be* Korean unless we have our independence."

Uncle said these things to me only yesterday. And yet, as soon as he'd said them, I felt as if I'd known them all along. All my life.

Sun-hee shakes her head and frowns. "More important than family?" she asks. But it's not one of her usual whiny little-sister questions. She's thinking hard, I can tell.

"Our duty to Abuji is important," I say. "It's a part of our culture. But if the Japanese have their way, someday there won't be any such thing as our culture. When Uncle works for independence, he works for the right to live as Abuji wants us to. . . . Do you see what I mean?"

I'm not as sure of myself as I'm trying to sound. It's so

confusing. Uncle acting like *chin-il-pa* when he's not . . .
Tomo, the son of an important Japanese official, helping a
resistance worker . . . Uncle disobeying Abuji in order to be
able to obey him one day. If I can't fully understand, how
can she?

I walk back toward her, reach out my hand so I can pull
her to her feet. "We'd better go in now," I say. "Sun-hee, we
shouldn't talk about this anymore, unless it's truly necessary.
And don't trust anyone. Not even Tomo. He helped us this
once, but it can't have been easy for him, and who knows if
he'll be sorry he did it."

She looks stunned. She hadn't thought about that. Poor
kid.

We go back inside, sit down, pretend to study. After only
a few moments, the megaphone blares. A neighborhood
accounting. At night.

They're almost always in the daytime. It's about Uncle, I
know it. They've raided his shop and now they're searching
for him.

Abuji looks at us. His face is calm but serious as well. He's
telling us to be calm, too.

Sun-hee leaves quickly to fetch Mrs. Ahn. We go outside
and line up in the street. So many soldiers—lots more than
usual. People are looking around, wondering.

We save a place for Mrs. Ahn. It's taking Sun-hee a while
to bring her out. Omoni turns to me. "You had better go
see—" she starts to say. But just then Sun-hee and Mrs. Ahn
hurry up to us.

I look at Sun-hee as she slips into line next to me. "I
couldn't find her at first," she whispers. "She didn't answer

the door, and then I finally found her in the garden." Sure enough, on the other side of me Mrs. Ahn is fussing about dirt on her hands, using a corner of her apron to wipe them.

We number off. Then the block leader starts talking. The usual spiel about His Majesty's Imperial forces. I'm dreading what he'll say next—about Uncle. He'll probably call him a traitor. I wish he'd get it over with.

"Metal!" the block leader says. "By order of the Emperor, the army is commandeering all household objects made of metal. It is needed for supplies, so His Majesty's Imperial forces can continue to spread his divine message to all people. Return to your homes and collect all your metal. You may keep a few things. Basic cooking tools. A shovel, an ax. Scissors and needles. Everything else, you must bring to your front gate."

Next to me, Sun-hee makes a choking noise, turns toward me, and grabs my arm. She looks so pale I'm afraid she might faint.

They want metal? What about Uncle?

Is he in danger?

Or has he gone into hiding for no reason?

No time to think about it now. Abuji sends me to the work area to gather up all the metal things there. Omoni goes into her bedroom to fetch the jewelry.

Outside, the soldiers are shouting up and down the street, yelling for us to bring all the metal things in bags.

Omoni comes out into the courtyard. She doesn't own much jewelry, but she needs both hands to carry it. Some silver bracelets and rings, a gold hair ornament, a necklace and a brooch. The last two were a wedding gift from

Abuji's parents—a silver dragon on the necklace and another one on the brooch.

Sun-hee seems almost frozen—she hasn't moved since we all came inside. But now she looks at Omoni. "Not the dragon," she whispers. Her lips are white. I remember when she was little, she always used to beg Omoni to let her wear the brooch. It was her favorite because the dragon has a little pearl ball in its claw.

"Bring me the bag, Tae-yul," Omoni says. Calm, like Abuji. I've already put a bunch of metal stuff in an old rice sack. She drops the jewelry in, a piece at a time. Clink, clink.

But not the brooch.

All of us are watching her. She turns away a little, raises the hem of her skirt, and drops the brooch right into her underwear. Then she smoothes her skirt down again.

Abuji makes a sound, sucking in air. He looks at Omoni for a long moment. She holds her head high. Finally, he nods. "Take the bag to the gate, Tae-yul," he says.

So I do. A military truck drives slowly down the street. Soldiers are taking bags and throwing them into the truck. Crash, clink, clang.

I watch as the truck drives away. Our things—Omoni's jewelry, my tools. No, *our* tools, mine and Uncle's.

Uncle. *Uncle.*

I take off, running as fast as I can toward town. Halfway there I remember that Abuji said I'm not supposed to leave the house, but it's too late now. I have to find out what's happening to Uncle.

When I reach the street where Uncle's shop is, I slow down a little. Nothing. No soldiers, no commotion. Uncle's shop is shuttered, looking like it always does when it's closed.

I go around to the back. No sign of any trouble.

What's going on?

I run all the way back home. Sun-hee is in the courtyard.

I don't mean to shout. But I can't stop the words from bursting out. "What happened? What have you done?"

15. Sun-hee

What have you done?

Tae-yul ran in, yelling at me. How could I have been so stupid, how could I have made such a mistake? Did I realize what I'd done?

He grabbed my arm hard, shaking me. Suddenly, our parents were there. Abuji pulled Tae-yul away, while Omoni stepped between us.

"Tae-yul! Calm yourself," Abuji said sternly. "What is the matter?"

"You heard her! Uncle has gone into hiding—she told him he had to, so he did!" Tae-yul wrenched himself free of Abuji's grasp, still panting. "He's gone! But she was wrong—they weren't about to arrest him. They only wanted the metal! I went to his shop—there was nothing going on there. No raid, nothing! How could she have gotten so mixed up? Why didn't she tell someone first?"

I still couldn't move, but my mind had started working again. I closed my eyes and thought back to the conversation with Tomo. What had he said, exactly? *Your uncle . . . a shame . . . not safe . . .* I couldn't remember anything clearly. The little things—he'd kept mentioning them. The little things made of wire—

Wire.

Metal wire.

That was what Tomo had been talking about. He'd been warning me that our metal things were about to be taken away. Maybe he thought that if we knew in advance, we could hide some things before it happened. But telling me straight out would have made him a traitor to the Japanese, his own people. He'd been telling me the only way he could—and I hadn't understood.

Behind my closed eyelids I could feel the heat of tears starting to rise.

When I opened my eyes, it felt like hours later, but Tae-yul's lips were still moving. I couldn't hear him; it was as if his voice were outside my hearing.

Abuji held up his hand. Tae-yul cut off his words abruptly. And I could hear again—a silence like iron, Tae-yul's heavy breathing the only sound.

Then Abuji said, "It does not matter how it happened. It is done now."

Tae-yul spoke between clenched teeth. "We have to get word to Uncle. We have to tell him it's all right, that he can come home. If we can send a message—if we tell the right people—"

Abuji shook his head. "I have already thought about this. It would be very dangerous to try to contact him. And it would take time—long enough so the authorities would hear of his untimely disappearance before he could return. If they were uncertain about his activities before now, they will surely know by then."

They again. The Japanese. Always the Japanese. My eyes

were dry now, and I didn't feel I was about to cry. I hardly felt anything at all.

Abuji paused and spoke again, each word careful and deliberate. "To be honest, I do not even know whom to get in touch with. My brother was cautious that way. He thought it best for me to know as little as possible."

"You mean, we're not going to do *anything?*" Tae-yul blurted out. "We're just going to—to live without him from now on?"

Abuji cleared his throat. "Tae-yul, you need to understand this. What your uncle was doing was very dangerous. It was only a matter of time. Sooner or later he would have been arrested or else forced to escape." He paused. "If he had been arrested, who knows what they would have done to him."

Abuji moved toward me and put one hand on my shoulder. I could see it there, although I barely felt it. He turned his head and continued speaking to Tae-yul. "He is safe now. Safer than he would be if he were here."

He was trying to comfort me, I could tell, trying to tell me that the rash and terrible thing I'd done wasn't so terrible after all. I wanted to believe him, but in my head I could still hear the echoes—*stupid, stupid, stupid. . . .*

Tae-yul didn't believe him either. He shuffled his feet impatiently, then lifted his arms and let them drop by his sides again. "When will he be able to come home?" he asked.

There was no answer.

When Tae-yul was a baby, he'd slept with Omoni and Abuji. A few years later, when I was born, I slept in my parents' room and he moved into Uncle's bedroom. That was how we always slept now.

As I went to bed that night, I realized that Tae-yul would have the whole room to himself. If I hadn't been so numb, I might have laughed. What a thing to think at such a time.

I undressed and lay down. In the darkness I began to feel things again. First, a huge dry lump in my throat. I swallowed and swallowed, trying to get rid of it. Instead, it swelled until I nearly choked on it. At long last the tears began.

I cried and cried. Not sobbing or gasping for air, but silently. Tears poured out of my eyes without stopping. When I was on my back, they ran into my ears. So I turned onto my stomach and let my pillow catch them all.

I wasn't making any noise, but a long time after everyone was in bed Omoni rose and tiptoed to my side of the room. She knelt down beside me, but I couldn't make myself turn toward her.

"Sun-hee," she whispered, "a mistake made with good in your heart is still a mistake, but it is one for which you must forgive yourself."

She reached out and smoothed my hair away from my hot, wet face. "Perhaps now you cannot. One day you will." She stroked my hair again, but after a long moment, when it was clear that I wasn't going to answer, she went back to her own bed.

I curled into a little ball, tight around the pain in my middle. Her words had only made me feel worse. Because the truth was, there hadn't been good in my heart.

There had been *some* good, of course. I was worried about Uncle; I didn't want anything bad to happen to him. But there were other things, too. *I* wanted to be the one to save him. *I* wanted to be the one with the important news, the

80

one who'd figured everything out. Not my parents. And especially not Tae-yul.

Instead of saving Uncle, I'd put him in terrible danger. When the Japanese found out he had left suddenly, they'd know for certain that he was a rebel, working for independence. If they found him, he'd be arrested, jailed for years . . . tortured . . . maybe even killed.

I wouldn't be able to forgive myself until Uncle came home safely.

But who knew when that would be?

16. Tae-yul

The next night, another neighborhood accounting. "A traitor among us!" the block leader shouts. Uncle's disappearance has been discovered. How did they find out so fast? They've been to the school and questioned Abuji. I know what he said—that he doesn't know where Uncle is. What else could he say?

The military police have raided Uncle's shop and found evidence of an illegal Korean newspaper. Uncle is now a criminal, wanted for treason against the Empire.

A house-to-house search. The soldiers spend the longest time at our house. We stand outside for nearly two hours, still there when everyone else has gone back to their homes.

At last the soldiers come out. We start to go inside. But the officer in charge of the search speaks to Abuji. "You are wanted for more questioning at police headquarters," he says. Then he nods at two other soldiers, who step forward to take Abuji by the arms.

But Abuji holds up his hands to stop them. "There is no need," he says. Quiet, like always. "I will come with you willingly."

We watch helplessly as he's taken away.

I can't keep still. I stand up a dozen times, go to the door, look toward the gate. Finally, I say to Omoni, "It's been a long time. I think I should go to the headquarters and see—"

"*No.*" She doesn't even let me finish my sentence. Her voice is like cold steel. "You are not to leave this house. Now sit down."

She never talks to me like that. I sit down meekly. No arguing with that voice.

Sun-hee and Omoni are sewing. I try to study, but I keep seeing Abuji's face. Bruised and battered, like Uncle's that time. I have to go back in my book again and again, rereading sentences I've just read.

We sit like that—the three of us, together in the middle of the room—for half the night. Omoni doesn't say we should go to bed—she doesn't even seem to notice we're there.

At last: footsteps outside the gate. I rush to the door.

Abuji is fine! Not a single mark on him. He looks surprised to see us still awake.

"They questioned me," he says. "I could not tell them anything, so they let me go."

I know it's thanks to Uncle. He told us almost nothing about his underground work. To protect us—all of us. If the authorities thought Abuji knew anything, they'd have beaten it out of him.

Omoni rattles around in the kitchen making tea for Abuji. She tells us to go to bed right away.

A million questions in my mind. I lie down on my side,

facing toward where Uncle usually sleeps. Right away I turn over onto my other side, but that doesn't help—I can still feel the empty space at my back.

I think I'm going to be awake all night—the room feels so cold without Uncle there. But I fall asleep almost the second I close my eyes. As if my mind needs somewhere to hide.

Guards are posted at our house, watching and following everyone in the family all day long. After about a week, they aren't there around the clock anymore, but they still come by several times a day. It makes us all nervous—we're never sure when a soldier might suddenly show up.

It seems impossible that our lives can go on with Uncle gone. But except for the soldiers, everything is back to normal. Sun-hee and I go to school, Abuji to work, Omoni keeps house.

Normal . . . but not normal. I think of Uncle all the time. We'd have heard if he'd been caught. So he must have escaped. But where is he? Is he alone? Is anyone helping him? Will he ever be able to come home?

It's so hard to get used to him not being around. I miss his stories, doing things with him in our workshop—most of all his little jokes, the way he always makes us laugh. Abuji never makes jokes. Our house feels so much quieter and sadder now.

At first I was angry at Sun-hee. But I couldn't stay that way, not for long. Not the way she looks now—pale, with circles under her eyes.

I try to forget about it, about what she's done. Abuji is right—it doesn't matter how it happened. Uncle is gone. That's what matters.

The day after Abuji went to the police station, Omoni tells

83

me to carve some bowls out of gourds from the garden. Our brass ones are gone, taken away by the Japanese.

I go out to the workshop. Most of the tools are gone, too. But we've kept an ax and a knife. I split the hard gourds in half, smooth the bottom halves with the knife, and scrape them with a piece of broken glass so they'll sit flat.

I spend most of the afternoon working. Sun-hee comes out before dinner to fetch the bowls. I hand her the stack, bottom side up, so she can see what I've done.

With the knife tip I've carved something on the underside of each bowl.

She frowns when she takes the bowls, almost turns them over, but then she sees it.

A faint circle, with a wavy line across it.

Sun-hee looks at it, then at me. And smiles. Small, but still a smile.

Weeks go by, then months. I'm surprised to find that sometimes I don't think about Uncle for hours, sometimes even all day. I feel guilty—it's strange to realize that I could get used to him being gone.

It's partly because we're all so busy with war activities. There's a new project at school. Once a week my classmates and I march into the hillside forests to gather pine roots. The roots are loaded into carts and taken away by the military. They use the resin to clean aircraft and weapons.

We all know what it means: Japanese supplies are low. Coal, oil—things like that. The war is using up everything too fast.

Splinters and scratches. Omoni works on my hands at night. First, she takes out splinter after splinter. Then she rubs herb stuff on the cuts and scratches.

Stickiness everywhere—the pine sap gets all over my clothes. And the smell, no matter how much I wash. Funny, I used to love the smell of fresh pine. Now I hate it.

One day at school, there's an announcement, an exciting one. The Japanese are going to build an airstrip just outside town!

I can hardly believe it. An *airstrip*—planes would actually land here! Teacher asks for volunteers to help build it. Mine is the first hand raised.

I talk to Abuji that night after supper. "I volunteered to help build the airstrip," I say.

Abuji sips his tea. It's not real tea anymore, it's herbs from the garden, but we still call it tea. "How often will you be called on to work there?" he asks.

I was afraid he'd ask that and I know he won't like the answer. "The work on the airstrip is to be done every day," I say slowly. "Anyone who volunteers will be excused from their studies until it's finished." I hold my breath and try not to look away from him.

He frowns. "Your education is important, Tae-yul."

I know what I want to say, but not how he'll take it. "Abuji, I do not mean to contradict you, but if the lessons were worthwhile, I would never even consider missing school."

Silence. He knows what I mean. My lessons: The sayings of the Emperor . . . The victories of the Imperial forces . . . The superiority of Japanese culture. *That's* what I'll be missing.

Is there a look of pain on his face? Or am I only imagining it? "In the evenings you will study kanji and reading with Sun-hee," he says.

Permission granted! I suck in my cheeks to keep from smiling. "Yes, Abuji. Thank you."

85

Later I think about it again. I wasn't imagining things—it *does* hurt him to know that my lessons aren't what I should be learning.

I realize something else. Why he's never punished me for not being a better scholar.

The same reason.

A few days later my new life as a worker begins. Every morning I march off with the other volunteers to the field where the airstrip is being built. We're given spades or shovels, then we dig and move dirt all day long, bossed by soldiers.

I didn't expect this. I thought we'd be supervised by our teachers. The soldiers are a lot crueler. Punishment isn't being struck with a bamboo cane across your legs but standing with the shovel held over your head. For a long time—hours, even. Some students get slapped hard in the face for working too slowly or not saluting respectfully enough.

I make certain never to be punished. If I am, Abuji will make me stop working at the airstrip, make me go back to school. I listen carefully, obey orders quickly. It's hard work, but it beats going to school.

Blisters. At night I sometimes wake from the pain. Omoni soaks rags, ties them onto my hands. Soon I have calluses instead of blisters. And then a thick layer of skin, tough as leather.

Two months after I start at the airstrip, I come home with a new badge on my collar: the Japanese flag with wings. Sunhee notices right away, raises her eyebrows at me, then at the pin. Asking but without words. She's still so quiet.

"All the volunteers got one," I say. I glance down at the

pin. "We're now members of the 'Japanese Youth Air Corps.' If airplanes ever land on the airstrip, the Youth Air Corps will be allowed to greet them. We might even get to clean the planes, or polish them, or whatever they do with them."

I look at her. "Just think—we'll be right there on the field, when the planes land and take off. And while they're here, I might get to see the inside of one—maybe even sit in the pilot's seat."

Sun-hee doesn't seem that impressed. But at least she says something. In a whisper. "That's good, Opah. Will the planes be coming soon?"

I shake my head. "Not soon—we have to finish the airstrip first. How do you expect planes to come here if they don't have anywhere to land?"

She doesn't know the first thing about planes.

17. Sun-hee (1943-44)

After Uncle left, I couldn't trust myself to speak. It seemed that my mouth and heart and eyes were all connected. When I opened my mouth to talk, my eyes would fill with tears. To keep from crying I had to close my mouth. So I didn't talk much.

But that was all right, really. To talk you have to think. And I couldn't think either. It was like being frozen—not outside, since my body still moved and did the things I needed it to do. But inside, everything—my mind, my feelings—was like ice.

No, that wasn't right either. Ice was cold, ice felt like something. This was nothing, a great big hole. When I turned my thoughts inside, there was nothing there.

It helped a little that my body was very busy. Tae-yul and some of his classmates were building the airstrip instead of going to school, and there were changes at my school, too. At least one full day every week was devoted to preparations for an invasion.

We'd been without a radio for more than a year now, so we heard nothing of this; we learned only what the Japanese officials wanted to tell us at the neighborhood accountings. But what they were having us do at school was a sign of their concern. It seemed that the Americans and their allies were pushing hard—so hard that the Japanese feared an invasion of Korea or even the islands of Japan.

My classmates and I were required to make huge piles of stones. If the enemy invaded the town, we were to pelt them with the stones. We filled hundreds of sandbags; the military took them away. It was hard work, but I was glad—the work made me tired enough to sleep at night. It was only after defense-preparation work that I slept well.

We sharpened bamboo poles—one for every student. These were stored leaning up against the courtyard wall. If the enemy advanced as far as the school, we were to take up the poles and bayonet them. We practiced driving a bayonet into a dummy made of straw that hung from a wooden framework.

"One soldier," Buntaro-san would say over and over again through the megaphone. He was the military attaché at this school, the position Onishi-san had held at my elementary school. "If three of you work together to bayonet just one soldier, you will be heroes to the Imperial forces. The Emperor will honor you personally. One soldier for every three students—that is all he asks."

Standing in line, waiting for my turn to bayonet the dummy, I looked around the courtyard. There we were in our worn-out uniforms, which used to be navy blue but had faded to gray. A hundred or so schoolgirls, some older than me but some two or three years younger, and I was only thirteen. With flimsy bamboo poles, most of which weren't even sharpened properly, we were to defeat the enemy invaders, with their guns and grenades and bombs.

Suddenly, I thought of Uncle. How I wished I could tell him about this. He'd have made some kind of funny joke. I tried to think of what he might say, but nothing came to me. I couldn't see the funny side, the way he would have. But I did manage a half-smile at one thing—it was the first time I'd thought of him without crying.

Jung-shin caught my eye, and I could see too that she was thinking how ridiculous this was. Just suppose she and I and another classmate were able to corner an American soldier. He'd have to be all by himself, unarmed, and weak enough to be overcome by three schoolgirls.

Even if that *did* happen, I was sure I wouldn't be able to do as Buntaro-san was commanding. Stabbing a man would be quite a different thing from stabbing a straw dummy.

I couldn't understand what the Japanese were thinking. Did they really believe we Koreans had been transformed somehow—that we were now Japanese? Didn't they know that we *wanted* the Americans to come to Korea and fight them?

But I was worried about something. I'd heard that the missionaries and other white people who had come to Korea couldn't tell the difference between Koreans and Japanese on sight. This astounded me. Both had black hair and dark eyes, it was true. But Japanese men, especially, were easy to tell apart from Koreans. They were much shorter, and their complexions were darker, more olive-toned. And the way they walked was different—stronger, almost arrogant.

Maybe the American soldiers would be like the missionaries. Maybe they wouldn't know the difference between Koreans and Japanese—they'd think we were all the same, like those black-haired people in the film.

One fall afternoon we were in the schoolyard, having bamboo-bayonet practice. We heard the drone of a plane approaching and waited for the usual all-clear siren, which meant that it was a Japanese plane and that there was nothing to worry about. But for the first time ever, no signal came.

We'd been drilled countless times on what to do if this happened. In seconds we had lined up and were marching back to our classrooms. There we crouched beneath desks and tables, as far away from the windows as possible.

The silence was eerie. Not one student cried or screamed. The engine noise grew louder and louder, and I braced myself, waiting for a bomb to hit the school. Now some of the girls had tears rolling down their faces. Others moved their lips in silent prayer. The girl next to me had fallen over in a faint. Oddly, this made me feel stronger. I didn't want to faint; I wanted to be aware, to see what happened.

But now the noise of the plane was growing fainter and fainter, and soon we could no longer hear it. There was no sound of an explosion, no firestorm. What did it mean?

The teacher crawled out from under her desk. She went to a window and slid it aside, looking out cautiously. Past her head, I could see a patch of sky.

It was snowing.

Not snowflakes. Paper. The sky was filled with falling paper.

We heard the all-clear signal, then Buntaro-san's voice in the courtyard, shouting through the megaphone.

"In your seats, everyone!" the teacher ordered. "Keoko, go out to the courtyard and find out what is going on."

I rushed outside. The yard was filled with students and teachers milling about in confusion. Quickly, I picked up one of the pieces of paper—it was a little folded leaflet—and tucked it into my waistband without looking at it.

Meanwhile, Buntaro-san was screaming into the megaphone. All students were to pick up the leaflets and bring them at once to the back of the school! No leaflets were to be left on the school grounds or even thrown into a waste bin! Every single one was to be burned!

The leaflet in my waistband scratched and tickled me all the rest of the day. I was terrified that someone would catch me with it, but for the first time in weeks my curiosity was stronger than my fear. I wanted to know what it said. If the Japanese didn't want us to read it, it had to be important.

Later I learned that the Youth Air Corps, including Tae-yul, had been sent throughout the town and into the surrounding hills to pick up the leaflets. There was a neighborhood accounting to announce that anyone caught with one of the leaflets would be severely punished. Soldiers went door to door and searched every home.

It all happened so quickly that not many people had a chance to read the leaflet. It was written in Korean, so most people couldn't have read it anyway. We all still spoke Korean at home, but only older people—those who'd learned to read before the Japanese occupation—could read it. Tae-yul had once told me that Abuji could read and write Hangul, the Korean alphabet. Abuji would be able to tell me what the leaflet said.

When I arrived home from school, Tae-yul met me in the courtyard. "Did you see it? Did you see the plane?"

I told him no, that we'd hurried inside.

"I saw it!" he said proudly. "It flew right over the airfield. Sun-hee, you should have seen how fast it went! And the pilot waggled his wings when he went over us, like he was waving!" You'd have thought he'd been flying the plane himself.

I showed him the leaflet I'd hidden. He grinned at me and pulled one out of *his* waistband.

Abuji came home and Tae-yul gave him the leaflets. He read one of them quickly, raising his eyebrows. Then he put them into the stove and burned them. He did it all slowly, deliberately. I thought he'd never get around to telling us what they said.

Finally, he turned to us. "The leaflets are from the Americans," he said, "signed by an army general—a man named MacArthur. He says it is known that the Korean people are not America's enemies, and he promises that Korea will never be bombed by American planes."

The Americans knew! They knew that Koreans weren't the same as Japanese!

Uncle's words to Tae-yul came back to me in a great rush—about how we Koreans weren't allowed to be Korean. What did it mean to be Korean, when for all my life Korea had been part of Japan?

It took the words of a man I'd never heard of—a faraway American—to make me realize something that had been inside me all along. Korean was the jokes and stories Uncle told us. It was the flag he'd drawn. It was the rose of Sharon tree Omoni had saved, and the little circle Tae-yul had carved on the bottom of the gourd bowls. Korean was the thoughts of Mrs. Ahn, in her own language, not someone else's.

And my thoughts, too. I was Korean—my thoughts were Korean.

I was so impressed by this idea that I went at once to the cupboard and fetched a tablet of paper and a pencil. From now on I would keep a diary. When Uncle came back, he'd want to know about things like the leaflets. And the bayonet practice. A diary would help me remember.

My first entry: "Paper fell from the sky today."

I looked at the line on the page and frowned. My handwriting was, as always, quite tidy. But it was in Japanese.

I couldn't write in Korean; I'd never been taught how.

Could Korean thoughts be written in Japanese?

The next night after dinner, I spoke to Abuji. "I would like to learn Hangul," I said. "Would you teach me?"

Abuji looked surprised for a brief moment. Then his eyelids dropped quickly and his expression grew blank. "The teaching of Hangul is illegal," he said quietly.

"Yes, Abuji." I bowed my head respectfully. "Illegal in school, but I was wondering—" I chose my next words carefully. "Does that mean it is also illegal in someone's house, where nobody else could see or hear?"

Again, there was a look of surprise on his face—one eyebrow raised. He was quiet for a long time, but I sat very still and waited.

At last he looked up and spoke slowly. "Sun-hee, it is not the right time. There are too many eyes around us just now." Pause. "But I promise one day to teach you Hangul."

I bowed and left the room, thinking about what Abuji had said.

Too many eyes. I understood this. The Japanese were watching us because of Uncle's escape. Not as closely as during the first few weeks, but still more than usual. We might be studying Hangul and soldiers might burst in on us. It was too dangerous.

I promise one day . . . One day? When? When would the Japanese let us have our own language back?

Still, it was a promise. Abuji almost never said "promise." When he said it, he meant it. But for the time being I had to write in my diary in Japanese.

I kept it faithfully, at least a line or two every day about the day's events. When nothing special happened, I wrote a little poem. Sometimes I tried to make these funny, as Uncle might like them that way:

> *Splash!*
> *A moment of clumsiness:*
> *My soup travels from the bowl*
> *through the air to my skirt.*
> *And I travel with it—*
> *to the shores of Omoni's disapproval!*

But often I could not keep the melancholy out of my words:

> *If I could choose to be anything,*
> *I would choose Wind.*
> *I would blow my way swiftly*
> *to wherever you are*
> *and hide myself*
> *among the leaves of the nearest tree.*

94

Omoni and Abuji never talked about Uncle. If Abuji knew anything about him, he never told us. It was almost worse than if he'd died. If he *were* dead, they'd have talked about him.

At least Tae-yul still talked about Uncle. To be honest, we didn't mention him often; it made us both too sad. But sometimes when I was out on the street with Tae-yul, I'd see his eyes darting about, searching people's faces. I knew he was looking for Uncle, just as I was. At those times it made me feel stronger to have Tae-yul nearby—to know we were thinking the same thoughts.

In early spring of 1944 our classes stopped entirely. We still reported to school every day, but all of our time was spent on preparations for an enemy invasion.

There had been no battles in Korea, yet the war was so much a part of our lives. Thousands of people had been separated from their families, forced to move to Manchuria and Japan to work for war industries. College students had to join the Imperial Army. Soldiers took not only rice and metal but anything edible or useful that they could get their hands on. Omoni worked harder and harder to put skimpy meals on the table. We weren't starving, but we never had quite enough to eat either.

And the mountains had changed color.

Our town was surrounded by mountains. Before the war those mountains had been covered with forests. When the Japanese took all the coal and oil for the war effort, we had to use wood for fuel. One after another, trees were chopped down, until at last there was hardly a tree anywhere. We used to be able to see green and pleasant slopes. Now they were brown, gray, dead.

We knew what had happened to the trees—they'd been burned. But we didn't know what had happened to many of the people in our town. One day they were there, and the next they were gone. Taken away by the Japanese—that much we knew. But to where?

One afternoon as we were building rock piles in the schoolyard, Buntaro-san took up the megaphone. "All girls sixteen years and older, report to the northeast corner. All girls sixteen and older. The rest of you, continue your work."

I was working with Jung-shin; she brought the rocks to me and I arranged them in neat piles. We were in the southeast corner of the yard and could hear everything.

When the older girls had lined up, the principal began speaking to them. "His Divine Majesty the Emperor is giving you girls a wonderful opportunity. There is great need for workers in Japan, in the textile factories making uniforms for the honorable members of the Imperial forces. You will be given a place to stay and ample food to eat. And a salary will be paid to your families here in Korea. It is a chance to help both the Empire and your own family! Who among you would like to volunteer for this noble cause?"

The job sounded too good to be true. We were all accustomed to figuring out the real meaning behind what the Japanese said or wrote. But I couldn't begin to guess what this announcement was truly about. Teenage girls could hardly be recruited as soldiers. Perhaps it was as the principal said; surely, it was true that Japan needed more factory workers.

I watched as a few of the older girls raised their hands. The principal actually *bowed* to those who stepped forward. "Look at these patriotic girls!" he said. "The Emperor and

96

their families will be so proud of them! Come, aren't there more of you who would like to join them in this endeavor?"

A few more girls came forward, but the principal wasn't satisfied. He gestured to Buntaro-san, who stepped up and shouted, "Twenty girls! The Emperor requests twenty loyal girls from our school. You must do your part!"

No one else volunteered beyond that first half dozen girls. Buntaro-san was getting angry. "If there are no more volunteers, I will choose them myself," he announced. He marched down the line and began pulling girls out one by one. "You and you—and you—"

One of those girls began to cry. Buntaro-san whirled around and hit her with his stick. "Shut up, you stupid girl! What do you have to cry about? Any sensible girl would be honored to serve the Emperor!"

There was silence throughout the schoolyard now. We'd all stopped our work and were watching. Buntaro-san dragged girl after girl out of line and shoved them toward the front.

Suddenly, Jung-shin gasped. Her older sister, Hee-won, had just been pulled from the line.

Hee-won immediately dropped to a bow before Buntaro-san. She started to say something, but he was already shouting at her. "Get up! Go join the others!"

Hee-won rose with a whimper and stumbled toward the front. But when she got there, the principal looked at her and frowned. He shook his head and sent her back to her place in line. "Not that one," he said to Buntaro-san. "Choose another."

Just then Buntaro-san seemed to realize that the rest of us were watching. "Back to work, all of you!" he yelled in a fury.

As we returned to our work, Jung-shin caught my eye, her face stunned and bewildered. Her hands trembled as she handed me the rocks. She seemed nearly faint with relief that her sister wouldn't have to leave home and go to Japan.

But why was that? No other girl had been sent back to the line. I could tell Jung-shin didn't know either; she looked as confused as I felt.

A terrible thought came to me. I tried to push it away, but that only seemed to make it hiss louder in my mind, like a snake coiling and baring its fangs until I could think of nothing else.

Hee-won had been spared as soon as the principal had seen who she was. Why would a girl be given such consideration?

It could mean only one thing.

Their father was *chin-il-pa*. A friend of the Japanese.

Jung-shin and her sister hurried away as soon as school was dismissed, and I went home on my own. I trudged heavily, as if my steps were weighed down by my thoughts.

There were things that made sense now. Why Jung-shin had been able to give me a rice cake when no one else had any rice at all; at the time, I'd been so excited to have *duk* again that I hadn't even wondered how she'd gotten it. Why she still had nice clothes, sometimes even new things, when everything I wore had been mended a dozen times. Maybe even why we always played at my house, not hers . . . perhaps her family worried that their association with the Japanese might somehow be discovered.

I hadn't thought about any of this very much before. There had been no reason for me to be jealous of Jung-shin.

98

If anything it had been the other way around—she respected me because my father was a scholar and hers only a banker, and because I was Class Leader every year. Now I saw things in a glaring new light that seemed to hurt my eyes.

With a start, I found myself thinking of Uncle. That day we'd visited him at his shop, when I thought he was acting oddly—it hadn't been just my imagination. Uncle must have known about Jung-shin's father, but he'd never told me. He must have been afraid I might say something to Jung-shin that would somehow give away his secret activities.

Could I be friends with someone whose family was *chin-il-pa?*

18. Tae-yul

Sun-hee meets me at the gate when I come home. She tells me what happened in the schoolyard. As usual I'm tired from the work at the airstrip. I only half-listen—until she mentions Hee-won's name.

Hee-won. Sometimes she comes to fetch Jung-shin at our house. She's my age, and really pretty. I feel my face growing a little warm.

Sun-hee doesn't seem to notice. Good. She whispers, "The principal took one look at her and sent her back to her place in line." No one is around to hear us, but I can tell she's afraid even so. "He told Buntaro-san to pick someone else."

I think for a moment. Then I say, "They have no brother."

"No brother—" She stops. Thinking instead of asking.

I choose my next words carefully. "Their father must feel that there's no one but himself to watch out for his family."

"But does that mean—do you think he could be—" She

swallows. Like me, she can't say it. Can't say the words *chin-il-pa*.

Suddenly, I pound the gate, cursing under my breath. "Damn! Damn the Japanese and this stinking war!"

Her mouth opens, then closes again. But there's still shock in her eyes.

It's wrong to scare her even more. I try to speak calmly. "It won't be easy for Jung-shin, wondering if people might guess the truth," I say. "You should be kind to her. Just be careful of—of what you say when you're with her."

She nods but still looks scared. I don't know what else to say.

Later I hear that those girls weren't even allowed to go home and say goodbye to their families. They were taken by truck straight to the train station. After that probably a train to the coast, and a boat to Japan.

And then what? A factory somewhere, sewing uniforms?

Maybe.

It's a warm spring night, the house dark and quiet. Everyone's in bed. Suddenly, there are loud voices at the gate. Before we can even get up off our mats, half a dozen soldiers burst into the courtyard. They turn on the electric light and shove open all the doors. I blink and squint—I can hardly see.

"Up, all of you," their leader orders. "Stand there, together, against the wall."

Shivering in our nightclothes, even though it's not cold. We gather around Abuji. Omoni's arms are crossed in front of her body. She's in her nightgown. Why won't they at least let her cover herself?

The leader stays with us while his men search every room in the house. They open cupboards, throw things around, overturn furniture, lift the straw floor mats.

After a few minutes Abuji clears his throat. "If the honorable officer would be so good as to tell me what he is seeking, perhaps I could be of assistance in locating it."

"Treasonous writings," the officer answers curtly. "Writings that express lies and slander against His Divine Majesty's benevolent presence in this country. And we need no assistance. If such writings are here, we will find them—you can be sure of that."

Beside me Sun-hee stiffens suddenly. I move my hand to take hold of her arm. She's trembling. I squeeze her arm a little, trying to calm her.

Treasonous writings? Are they looking for copies of Uncle's newspapers? There aren't any here, I know that for sure. Right after he left I looked all over the house a dozen times. I never even found a scrap of one. Besides, they'd searched the house themselves back then. Do they think he still contacts us? For the first time I'm *glad* he hasn't kept in touch with us—if he had, they might find him somehow. . . .

One by one, the soldiers come back into the courtyard. They're all holding papers. They put them down on the table before the leader. I glance down quickly. Mostly Abuji's work, but also Sun-hee's diary. Is that why she's worried? Surely nothing she's written can get us in trouble—she's only a girl. . . .

The officer picks up the papers and looks over them quickly. Documents and lesson plans for Abuji's school. But the officer doesn't care about these—he looks at them, then crumples them and tosses them on the floor.

Finally, he reaches for Sun-hee's diary. He flicks through the pages. Sun-hee clutches at her nightshirt, just like Omoni.

The officer looks up. "Whose stupid scribblings are these?" he asks abruptly.

Sun-hee answers at once. "Mine," she says. I'm surprised by her voice—it's strong, not shaky. And she's stopped trembling.

He sneers. "Idiotic thoughts written in a beautiful hand," he says. "Do not waste the glory of fine kanji on such nonsense—it is a crime against our Divine Emperor. You are fortunate that I will grant leniency this one time. Any more of this and I will not be so merciful."

He hands the diary to another soldier and makes a brusque gesture. The soldier takes the diary to the kitchen and throws it into the stove.

Sun-hee takes one step forward. I pull her back.

The officer finishes his inspection of the papers. He tears the last few into shreds. "We know that this town breeds a worm of treason!" he shouts. "We will hunt it down and grind it under our heel! All of you have been warned—if we find later that you knew anything of this treason, you will suffer the same fate as the traitor himself!"

Then he stomps out in fury, his men behind him.

The gate clangs shut. Sun-hee breaks free of my grasp and runs to the stove to try to save her diary. She reaches right into the fire.

Too late. There are only a few burned scraps of paper left. She kneels on the floor, holding them, Omoni next to her with a wet rag, wiping away the soot and ashes. Sun-hee's fingertips are turning red, starting to swell. It must hurt, but she doesn't cry. I pace and clench my fists, wishing there were something I could do.

Abuji comes over, his face worried. He watches Omoni tend to Sun-hee but doesn't say anything. He just stands there.

Seeing him like that makes me remember one of Uncle's stories from years ago, when he'd been hurt, after the Olympics. He couldn't work for a few weeks, so he stayed home. Sun-hee and I loved that—he was always around to tell us stories.

"My father—your grandfather—was a great scholar," Uncle had said. He was resting on his mat. Sun-hee and I were sitting on the floor to one side. "He devoted his entire life to studying. It took him many years and many attempts, but late in life he finally passed the difficult examinations and was appointed a scholar in the royal court.

"I was only a small boy, but I remember well how proud he was the day he put the jade button in his topknot. The button meant that he had passed the examinations. He let me touch it just once—to feel how smooth and round it was." Uncle smiled, a sad smile, then shook his head.

"Only a few weeks later the Japanese ordered all men to cut off their topknots and to wear their hair short, in the Japanese style. They said topknots were too Korean. Your grandfather would not do it. He had worked too hard for the jade button."

He looked away from us. At nothing. Like he was seeing something inside his head, a place or a time far away. His voice seemed to come from far away, too.

"One day three soldiers came to the house. They burst in without being invited and found my father in his room. Two of them held him down while the third one cut off his top-knot. And one of them stole the jade button.

"I was young, only four or five years old. I hid behind my mother's skirts—so frightened! I wanted to help somehow, but what could I do?" He shook his head again.

"But it wasn't enough, just to cut off his beautiful top-knot. One of them took a big handful of hair and threw it into the kimchee pot. He stirred it for a while, and all the time he and his friends were laughing . . ." Uncle's voice was so angry that he had to stop speaking for a few moments.

The kimchee pot. Every Korean home has one. A big ceramic pot sunk into the floor of the courtyard, so deep a man can almost stand inside. The pot keeps the spicy pickled cabbage from freezing during the winter. The kimchee is scooped out with a huge wooden ladle. The pot is always carefully covered because anything that falls in is hard to get out. Strands of hair—it would have been impossible to get them all out.

"But where was Abuji?" I asked. "He was a lot older than you—maybe he could have helped." Abuji is ten years older than Uncle.

Uncle frowned. "I think he was there too, but maybe not. Maybe he was at school—I don't remember.

"For weeks afterward my mother had to pick hair out of the kimchee. She tried to do it without my father seeing, but no matter how careful she was, there was sometimes still hair in the servings of kimchee. And every time this happened, my father could not eat.

"A few months later, he took ill and died. I do not remember what illness he had, but it does not matter. He died of a broken heart."

104

I remember Uncle's eyes glittering with pain and anger. I remember something else, too. How I'd felt hearing about Abuji, the way he'd done nothing to help. Back then I couldn't understand it. Why hadn't he done something?

Those soldiers tonight, tearing apart our house. And me? I'd stood there, frozen. I hadn't done anything—I hadn't even *said* anything. And I'm three years older than Abuji was then.

I know now. What could he have done? What could any of us do?

19. Sun-hee

When the officer asked, "Whose scribblings are these?" I'd answered at once. And right at that moment I hadn't felt afraid. I'd felt proud—proud that those were *my* words on the pages he was holding.

Now all the words I'd written for so many months were lost. My thoughts and feelings—they were a part of me, and it was as if that part had burned up in the stove, too. There was an empty space inside me where those words had been.

Besides, I'd been keeping the diary especially for Uncle. It was going to be sort of a present for him. And now it was gone. Would I fail at everything I tried to do for him?

After the soldiers left, no one said anything about what had happened. Omoni wrapped my burned hand, and we all went back to bed. But a few moments later, I heard Abuji's quiet voice. "Sun-hee, I am sorry about your writing."

In the dark I could feel my heartbeat speed up. My diary wasn't exactly a secret; I often wrote in it in the evenings when we were all in the sitting room together. But I'd never shown it to anyone and never realized that Abuji had noticed me working on it.

I felt a pulse of pride in my throat; I swallowed hard and managed to reply. "Thank you, Abuji. But it was nothing, really."

"No," he answered. "It was not nothing." He paused a moment, so his next words seemed to fill up the darkness. "But do not forget, Sun-hee—they burn the paper, not the words."

I woke the next morning with Abuji's words in my head. I started a new diary that very day; not even the pain of my blistered fingers could stop me.

> You burn the paper but not the words.
> You silence the words but not the thoughts.
> You kill the thoughts only if you kill the man.
> And you will find that his thoughts rise again
> in the minds of others—twice as strong as before!

Abuji was right. While I couldn't remember all of the diary entries, I was able to recall many of them, especially the poems. The pages were filled even faster than before, old words and new ones mixed together. I had that Japanese officer to thank for making me more determined than ever to write things down.

I realized something else, too. I thought about Abuji's promise to teach me Hangul one day. And now I knew exactly when that would be: when the Japanese no longer ruled Korea. When we were our own country again.

For that to happen, *the Japanese had to lose the war.* If they won, they'd be here forever. I thought back to the airdrop of leaflets—how glad I'd been to find out that the Americans knew that Koreans and Japanese weren't the same. I remembered hoping the Americans would come fight the Japanese and throw them out of our land. But I hadn't realized until now what it would mean to have them gone.

If the Japanese lost the war, Uncle could come home. If they lost, Abuji could be principal of his own school. We could learn Korean history. We could use our real names again!

And Abuji could teach me the Korean alphabet.

How could an alphabet—letters that didn't even mean anything by themselves—be important?

But it *was* important. Our stories, our names, our alphabet. Even Uncle's newspaper.

It was all about words.

If words weren't important, they wouldn't try so hard to take them away.

20. Tae-yul

A neighborhood accounting. It's chilly outside. I hope we won't have to stand around too long.

The block leader takes the count. Then he hands the megaphone over to an army officer who starts shouting about Japanese victories at sea.

"The flower of Japanese youth has blossomed into victory!" His voice is excited. "A Special Attack Unit of the Divine Imperial forces has inflicted terrible damage on the enemy fleet. Our military leaders are geniuses! And the young men who serve under them are heroes in the truest sense of the word!"

Now he tells a story from the past. Something that

happened centuries ago. I'm tired of learning Japanese history, but this story is interesting.

". . . an enemy navy invading from the west. More than three thousand powerful ships sailed across the sea, determined to land on our shores. But just before they reached the coast, there was a terrible storm—a typhoon! The wind raged and battered at their sails, and every single enemy ship foundered and sank. It was a *kamikaze*—a divine wind, a sign that our people are indeed favored by Heaven.

"The Emperor has honored the heroes of today with this glorious memory of the past. The pilots of the Special Attack Unit are to be known as kamikaze. They are the divine wind that will blow us to victory over the white devils!"

Pilots! The Special Attack Unit are pilots who fly airplanes!

"The kamikaze have made the ultimate sacrifice. They displayed the utmost in skill, and their bravery is all but impossible to imagine! No enemy will be able to withstand such power . . ."

He talks about how the sickly pale Americans cowered before the courageous kamikaze. He says the same thing a dozen different ways. But for once I don't mind. As long as he's talking about airplanes and pilots, I'll keep listening.

Then he says something I can hardly believe.

The kamikaze pilots flew their planes toward the Americans' ships. Each plane was equipped with bombs. The kamikaze deliberately crashed into the ships so their bombs would explode and cause maximum damage.

The kamikaze are commanded by their leaders to fly straight to their deaths.

They're suicide pilots.

I'm amazed at their bravery. It's one thing to know you might die in a battle—but *choosing* to die is something else, something special.

I do everything I can to find out more about the kamikaze. I read the endless stories about their bravery in the newspapers Abuji brings home. I even start talking to a guard whose regular beat is our street. His name is Shinagawa-san, but I always think of him as "Spade-face" because his face is so flat. He wanted to be a pilot but was disqualified—poor vision. When he tells me that, I quickly look down the street toward a shopfront with signs. To make sure I can read something far away.

Spade-face talks about how tough it is for the kamikaze to hit their targets. They fly their planes hundreds of meters above the sea, hidden by cloud cover. "Just imagine," he says. "They come out of the clouds and have to dive at once, before the enemy spots them and starts to fire. From that height the targets look no bigger than grains of rice! Once a plane is in a high-speed dive, it's almost impossible to direct its course. Can you imagine the skill?"

Only the best pilots are chosen for these missions. The kamikaze are treated like princes. They get the best of everything the Imperial forces can offer—the best food, the best accommodations. Their final meal before a mission is rice with red beans, a grilled bream, and *sake*.

Rice with red beans is a dish Koreans eat, too, for special celebrations. I haven't had it in a long time, but I still remember. The little red beans turn dark purple as they cook—when I was little, that always seemed like magic to me. The white rice is dotted with bits of color. Delicious—those beans hiding in the middle of a mouthful of rice.

I love fish. But there hasn't been any in the marketplace

for ages. Not since Pearl Harbor. Every boat and ship has been taken for the military.

Sake is rice wine, like our Korean *sool*. Spade-face tells me that the pilots each drink three cups of sake. They bow before drinking each one. First toward the shrine on the base. Then to the Emperor, in the direction of the palace. And the last drink for their families—they bow toward their hometowns.

Then they march out onto the airstrip to their planes. The whole base salutes them as they fly off.

I pretend it's me drinking sake, heading out onto the tarmac, and then taking off. Nothing but air underneath me and my plane.

21. Sun-hee (1945)

It seemed as if the war would never end. Day after day of too much hard work, not enough food, constant exhaustion— and no chance to make or do anything beautiful. If a war lasts long enough, is it possible that people would completely forget the idea of beauty? That they'd only be able to do what they needed to survive and would no longer remember how to make and enjoy beautiful things?

I was determined not to let this happen to me. At school every day, while I was working with my hands, I let my mind float away to think of something beautiful. The dragon pin, buried safely in the backyard; the way the little pearl ball shone, white but with a hundred unnamed colors gleaming. How the row of rose of Sharon trees had looked when in full bloom, each flower like an open mouth, singing. Or the mountains outside town—how they used to turn green a little at a time in the spring, the color climbing higher with each warm day.

I was afraid that if I didn't take time now to remember these things, I'd wake one day unable to recall them at all.

Jung-shin had avoided me ever since the incident in the schoolyard with her sister. We hadn't spoken even once, and this left a large, ragged hole in my life.

The days of defense-preparation work without her company were truly miserable. And as unhappy and uncomfortable as I felt, I could see whenever I glanced at her that she felt a hundred times worse. Her shoulders were always slumped and her eyes dull.

What Jung-shin's father did was the responsibility of the whole family; her father's shame was hers as well. That was why she couldn't face me.

I was sure she hadn't known her father was *chin-il-pa* before the day when I guessed, for she had seemed completely bewildered. I thought again of Uncle—how he'd never mentioned anything about Jung-shin's family.

Now I thought I knew why. I hadn't known then what Uncle was doing, nor had Jung-shin known what her father was doing. We were just two girls playing together. That must have been what Uncle had thought.

It was what I thought, too.

After school one day I rushed out and found the popcorn man. If he was anywhere in town, he was easy to find; you just followed the sound of the loud banging noises—the popcorn inside the cannon. I bought a bag, then hurried to a street corner Jung-shin would pass on her way home.

Soon she came along, walking slowly, with her head down.

She saw me standing there and her steps slowed even more. "Hello, miss," I called as she approached. "I hear you are good at cat's cradle. I would like to learn some new patterns. Don't worry, I can pay for the lesson." And I held out the bag of popcorn.

It was a wonderful sight, the way her eyes instantly regained their sparkle. Right away she began to play along. "Well, I don't know," she said, striking a contemplative pose. "I am very good at cat's cradle, and I'm not sure if one bag of popcorn is enough payment."

"Who said anything about one bag?" I said indignantly. "Some of this is for me, you know! I was offering *half* a bag!"

We laughed together, and I knew in that moment we could still be friends.

One evening late in winter Tae-yul asked to speak to Abuji alone. After supper Omoni and I immediately rose from our seats and left the room. We took the dishes to the back of the house under the eaves and washed them there, so the men would have some privacy. I was dying to know what Tae-yul had to say; I couldn't remember any other time that he'd asked to talk to Abuji privately.

There was quiet in the house for a little while, but as we were finishing the dishes we heard Abuji's voice. He was shouting. "What do you mean by this? You would deliberately disobey my express command?"

I was stunned—Abuji never shouted. Omoni immediately covered her ears with her hands and hissed at me to do the same. Reluctantly, I raised my hands to my ears. I knew it was rude to eavesdrop, but I couldn't help it: I covered my ears without completely blocking my hearing.

I couldn't hear the words—only quiet, then more shouting. They argued for a long time—long enough for my legs to cramp. At last there was silence. Omoni cautiously lowered one hand. Then she told me to empty the water basin while she took the dishes back to the kitchen.

"Yobo, Sun-hee," Abuji called in a stern voice. I dropped the basin and hurried inside.

Abuji was pacing back and forth in great agitation. Tae-yul had obviously just bowed to him; he was on his knees on the other side of the low table. Unhappiness seemed to fill the space between them, the whole room. Following Omoni in, I took only one step past the threshold and stood next to the sliding door, making myself as small as I could.

"Tae-yul has something to say," Abuji said.

Tae-yul swiveled on his knees and bowed his head to the ground toward my mother. Then he raised his head but kept his eyes down as he spoke.

"Omoni, today I enlisted in the Imperial Army. I leave for training in Seoul tomorrow."

My legs turned to paper. I grabbed for the door frame to keep from falling as Omoni cried out. "Why, why? You're too young—how—"

Tae-yul's face was pale, but his voice was steady. "I volunteered."

At this Omoni threw her apron over her face and collapsed, sobbing wildly. Abuji thrust out his hands in anger and shouted, "Look at her! Look what you have done to your mother!"

Tae-yul rose to his feet and bent over her. "Omoni, please," he whispered.

This was an old trick of Uncle's. When we were younger, crying over some small hurt or disappointment, Uncle would lower his voice and speak to us in a whisper. We had

113

to stop crying in order to hear what he said. It always worked, and now here was Tae-yul doing it, as if he were the adult and Omoni the child.

It worked this time as well; Omoni stopped crying and sat up. Tae-yul bowed before her again.

"I ask all of you to try to understand," he said. "The war is going badly for the Japanese. We know this—we can see it everywhere. They talk a lot about those kamikaze successes, but you can tell from that very tactic how desperate they are. The soldiers at the airstrip don't even have ammunition for many of their guns anymore. One more soldier, and an unwilling one at that, isn't going to make a difference in the outcome. The Japanese are losing. It's only a matter of time.

"But if I join the army, things will be much better for you. Families of volunteers receive rice rations and other considerations. Look at Sun-hee's clothes," he said bitterly, glancing over at me. "It's a wonder they hold together now—there are more mending stitches than cloth. They'll give you clothing, better food—they'll treat you better."

He was speaking to Omoni; he'd probably said all this to Abuji earlier. "I'm eighteen years old now. I'm not a child anymore—I need to help the family the best way I can."

Omoni stared at him. "And what help will you be to us if you die?" she asked quietly.

I knew what she was thinking. We'd heard rumors that Korean recruits were sent in at the start of any battle, to clear the way for the Japanese soldiers behind them. The Koreans were always the first to die. If Tae-yul were sent into battle, he'd be in the front line. . . .

For the first time Tae-yul shifted uncomfortably. "It's a real possibility that the war will be over soon. I'll have several weeks of training before . . . before they send me any-

114

where. Perhaps the war will have ended by then. . . ." His voice trailed off.

Omoni shook her head dazedly. Abuji had stopped his pacing and was standing with his shoulders bowed.

It was impossible to even imagine Tae-yul disobeying our parents in this way yet here it was, happening before my very eyes. And for what reason—to join the army and fight on behalf of the Japanese!

Suddenly, I was shouting. "You—you pig head! Don't you know I'd rather have a thousand patches in my clothes than lose my brother?"

In the next instant I saw the shock on all their faces. I was a girl, a younger sister—I had no right to express my opinion. But I didn't care. Omoni and Abuji weren't going to do anything—they weren't even going to try to stop Tae-yul, so it was up to me.

In the brief silence that followed I realized I didn't know what they *could* do. Lock him in his room?

It was so cruel. All of it—the occupation, the war, Uncle in hiding, Tae-yul going into the army . . . I needed to get out of that room; the unfairness of it all was choking me. I whirled and bolted out of the house.

I ran out into the garden, all the way to the back, dropped to my knees and slammed my hand against the stone wall. Over and over I struck it in fury, hardly knowing what I was doing.

In the midst of my frenzy my wrist was grabbed from behind and held in an iron grip.

I wrenched it free and turned around. Tae-yul was standing there.

"Don't talk to me," I snarled, raising my hand toward him.

115

"Shut up, you stupid girl, and listen," he said roughly.

I was so stunned by his rude manner that I froze as I was, my hand in the air and my mouth open.

Tae-yul knelt beside me. "I'm sorry I spoke to you like that—it seemed like the only way to get your attention." His voice was gentle now. "There's more that I haven't told our parents. But I want to tell you because—because I want someone to know the truth."

I lowered my hand but said nothing.

He leaned toward me and spoke softly. "Sun-hee, Uncle is still alive and still working for the resistance."

22. Tae-yul

Today a schoolboy . . . tomorrow a soldier. Just like that. I can hardly believe how it happened, but at the same time I remember every last thing.

It starts out like any other day, working at the airfield as usual. In the late afternoon, all of us line up to turn in our spades. A military policeman stands by the tool shed, talking to the officer in charge of the airfield. Both of them are looking at me. My stomach lurches a little.

One of the guards takes my spade from me and tells me to report to the officer, who tells me to go with the policeman.

The policeman has a *car*. He waves at me to get in on the passenger side, starts the engine, and drives us off toward town. I can hardly believe it. Me, riding in a car!

I'm surprised by how bumpy it is—I imagined it would be smoother. But we're going so fast! We zip past my classmates, lining up again to march back to school. Their mouths hang wide open when they see me.

While I'm in the car I almost forget that feeling in my stomach. My elbow is on the edge of the open window so I can stick my hand out, the wind blowing through my fingers.

But when we arrive at the police station, the bad feeling comes back, twice as strong. The policeman takes me to a room and leaves me there. A table and two chairs. One small window with bars. I don't know if I'm supposed to sit down, so I stay standing, wondering why I'm there and getting more nervous all the time. It's the military police—it can't be anything good. . . .

Finally, two cops come in—the one who drove me and an officer, tall for a Japanese, with bars and badges on his uniform. The driver stands by the door. The officer sits at the table and points to the other chair.

So I sit down across from him. I'm glad to sit—the funny feeling in my stomach is making my knees wobble a little.

The officer starts to talk. At first he sounds just like my teachers. Or the principal at our school. How much Japan does for Korea—roads, factories, schools . . . How Korea is such an important part of the Empire . . . How most of its citizens are grateful for the divine leadership of the Emperor.

At last he gets to the point, and I'm there ahead of him. I know exactly what he's going to say. I'm still scared, but at least I'm not surprised.

"A few citizens have proved to be less than grateful," he says. "They are liars and cowards who slander His Divine Majesty's Imperial presence in this country. There are only a few of them, but their voices are like the rotten spot on an apple. If they are not stopped, the rot will spread."

Uncle. He's talking about Uncle.

"Your uncle is among them," he continues.

I feel a flash of satisfaction, knowing I guessed right. Stay one step ahead of him, that's what I have to do. But I can't guess what he'll say next. And I'm afraid for Uncle.

Don't let him see how you feel, I warn myself. So I keep my face steady, my eyes on his hands on the tabletop. He has them clasped together. They look strong, with big knuckles. I never thought before that even hands can look cruel.

He's still speaking. "He is obviously a very intelligent man, your uncle. A man who loves his country." A smile, like he's my friend. "We need men like him in our fight against the white devils. We think he would find it most rewarding to use his skills and talents on behalf of the Emperor."

Inside myself I almost laugh. Uncle, working for the Emperor! The officer doesn't know what a funny thing he just said.

He waits a moment, like he wants me to say something. I don't. So he goes on. "At present, your uncle is, you might say, a problem for us. We wish him no harm—we wish only for a chance to speak with him, to help him see how his slanderous activities hurt progress and success in this country."

Then he furrows his brow and gives this fake sigh. "Unfortunately, not all of my colleagues admire your uncle as I do," he says, his voice full of regret. "There are those who feel it would be better to simply . . . eliminate him. They do not agree with my assessment that perhaps he can be re-educated."

Now he leans forward a little, like he's sharing a secret with me. "I have managed to convince them to give me a chance. To bring in your uncle so we can speak with him. If this does not work—" He stops. Doesn't need to finish the sentence.

"That is why I have invited you here today," he goes on. Invited me—he's being funny again. Like I had a choice. "I am in need of your assistance. Your uncle would hardly trust a message from me and my colleagues. But if you were to convince him to come speak with us—and give him my word that he would not be harmed—well, you are his nephew. He would trust you."

He leans forward even farther and lowers his voice. "We have ways that a message might be delivered. With luck it would reach him and enable us to set up a meeting. With you first, of course. And then you would bring him to us."

He's done talking. He leans back and waits for me to say something.

How long does it take for a hundred thoughts to go through your brain? Less than a second? A second and a half? *You would bring him to us.* What a lie. They'd be waiting to arrest Uncle as soon as he came to meet me.

I'll never help them do it. Not in a thousand years. But I can't let this officer know what I'm really thinking—or feeling. Anger. Such anger, that he called Uncle—the bravest man I know—a coward.

I have to find a way not to do it. But he's not really asking me. He's *telling* me. It's a command. Something I can't refuse—something I *have* to do.

They're doing it again. Taking whatever they want. Grandfather's hair, Omoni's jewelry, Sun-hee's diary. My bicycle. And we can't do anything to stop them.

Now it's Uncle they want. And they want me to stand there and do nothing again.

This time, I *have* to do something.

But what can I do? By myself, against an officer and his men—against a whole military police force. Against a whole government, really. They can make me do anything—take me from the airfield, from our home, even from my bed at night. . . .

Unless—

Unless I'm not there.

What about that? What if they couldn't find me?

I can't just run away—where would I go? And besides, they'll probably catch me before I even leave town.

All those thoughts—in so little time. I'd bowed my head when the officer stopped speaking, like I was ashamed of Uncle. Just to buy a few more seconds before I have to say something. Head down, thinking, thinking . . .

Leaving town—how would I go? On a train—Sung-kwon's brother left on a train. . . .

And in that instant the words come easily.

"Sir, I am honored that you should ask for my assistance. My uncle's absence has indeed caused my family much concern. However, I regret that I cannot be of help to you. I must tell you that I have volunteered to be part of His Majesty's Imperial forces. I leave tomorrow, to do my part in battle for his divine cause."

I don't know what I'm going to say before I say it. It's almost like someone else has spoken. It doesn't even feel like I'm lying. Before, whenever I lied I felt uncomfortable inside, knowing I wasn't telling the truth. But this time is different.

It's more like acting—becoming someone else, talking in a voice that isn't mine. I'm surprised at how easy it is. This is how Uncle did it, in his shop. Acted friendly toward the

Japanese, when all the while he was working against them.

The officer's face looks as surprised as I feel. Then upset, disappointed—that his plan isn't going to work. But only for an instant. He has to act pleased that I've volunteered for the army. He congratulates me on my excellent choice and blathers on about the army for a little while. Finally, he dismisses me.

I go straight to the army enlistment office. On the way I think it's almost funny. Both of us acting. Him like he really wanted to help Uncle, me like I really wanted to help him.

I register my age as eighteen. It's not a complete lie, because of the way we count our age, which is different from the way the Japanese count. Koreans are one as soon as we're born. Korean-style, I really *am* eighteen.

I tell them I want to enlist immediately. No one asks any questions. The Japanese army needs men desperately. They're taking almost anyone who volunteers.

A physical exam, then instructions to report to the train station the next day. I walk away slowly. Each step brings me closer to home. To the moment when I'll have to tell my family.

Everything is so inside out. I believe in Uncle and in the things he believes in. I'd do anything not to betray him. Anything. Even join the army of his sworn enemy.

I think of all this again, there in the garden with Sun-hee. Then I take a deep breath and start to tell her about it.

23. Sun-hee

Tae-yul and I talked in the garden for a long time. He told me everything that had happened in the police station. "Do

121

you know what this means about Uncle?" he asked. "They said it themselves—they said, 'Your uncle is a problem for us.' That means his work has been successful, Sun-hee—that he's still printing the newspaper. And it must be reaching hundreds of people. Maybe thousands. Even if—if something were to happen to me, it's of no importance compared to what the independence movement would suffer if Uncle is arrested."

He looked at me fiercely. "If they catch him, they'll kill him. The paper he prints—the truth in words—it must hurt the Japanese as much as a thousand guns."

In a single day, he seemed to have become so much older. "Oh, Opah," I whispered. "Isn't there any other way?" But I knew if there were, he'd have thought of it already.

He shook his head. "It's possible that their plan wouldn't work, that Uncle wouldn't let himself get trapped. But I can't take the risk."

He reached out and put his hand on my shoulder. "I'm sorry to burden you with this knowledge, Sun-hee," he said. "I don't want to tell Abuji. I'm his only son. I'm sure he feels that—that my life is worth more than Uncle's."

It was a staggering thought—to weigh the lives of two people I loved against each other, to decide which was worth more. For a moment I was glad it was not me having to make such an evil choice, and in the next moment, I was ashamed of my cowardice. I wiped away a few tears with the back of my hand and tried to compose myself.

"Opah, is there anything I can do?" It seemed so empty, my pitiful offer of help. What could a schoolgirl like me possibly do?

"Yes, Sun-hee, there is one thing. I'll be allowed to write letters, but I'm sure they'll be censored. I won't be able to put down the truth as I see it. I'm counting on you to read between my words and uncover their true meaning. It would mean a lot to me to know that you'll try to understand what I really want to say."

Such a small thing. I felt ashamed again and, worse than that, helpless. Here was Tae-yul, risking his life to save Uncle . . . and I could do nothing for either of them.

Maybe, at least, I could make Tae-yul smile, take that awful heavy look out of his eyes. Like Uncle would have. "Yes, all right," I said. "But please try to write legibly—your handwriting is terrible at times."

He looked surprised for the briefest instant, then burst out laughing when he realized I was joking. "I beg your pardon, O Queen of Kanji," he replied. "I cannot promise that my handwriting will meet your absurdly high standards, but I'll do my best."

"The queen has spoken," I said loftily. "Do not risk incurring my wrath." But I found that I couldn't stay very queenlike; I broke into giggles.

Now Tae-yul and I were both laughing. We laughed until we had to stop for lack of breath. Then Tae-yul looked at me and mimed a groveling bow, as if he were a lowly servant, and we were off once again. Soon we were both lying on the ground, weak from laughter.

Finally, Tae-yul stood and helped me to my feet. We walked back slowly toward the house.

At the back door we faced each other and bowed. A formal bow—a bow of farewell.

"Help our parents, Sun-hee," Tae-yul whispered. "And when you think of Uncle and me, don't be sad. Be proud."

The next morning he was gone.

———

I went to school and did the task we had been assigned for the day—filling sandbags? piling stones? Whatever it was, I did it automatically. At the end of the day I found myself in our courtyard with no memory of having walked home.

First Uncle, and now Tae-yul. I simply couldn't think about it—couldn't imagine what life would be like with both of them gone.

My feet took me the few steps to the room that had been theirs. I stood at the doorway and looked inside. Omoni had already tidied up. Everything was in its place: the sleeping mats out of sight in the low cupboard, books and a few old toys on the shelf.

I walked over to the shelf. There was Tae-yul's old top, worn down at the nib from all the spinning. He hadn't thrown it away. His books were there, too, including the primer with the Japanese alphabet—the one we'd used to choose our new names.

Suddenly, I longed to hold a book again. It had been weeks since we'd had regular classes at school. Abuji had offered to continue my kanji lessons at night, but after the hours of defense-preparation work, I was usually exhausted and went to bed early. Standing there in Tae-yul's lonely room, I realized how much I missed my studies—reading and writing most of all.

My diary—of course. I usually wrote in it just before bed. But there was no reason I couldn't write in it now.

I fetched it from the cupboard in the other bedroom and wandered out into the backyard. I ended up at Tae-yul's work area. Like his room, it looked a little forlorn—nearly all the tools were gone. Omoni hadn't cleaned it up yet, so it had more of the feeling that he'd just been there.

I sat on an old mat beside the little tree. The tree wasn't doing very well. We'd kept it covered up for days at a time, while the soldiers were searching for Uncle. It had lost a lot of leaves back then and hadn't grown them all back. But it was still alive.

My diary had a lot of entries about Uncle now. No one reading them would know they were about him, but I'd been thinking of him when I wrote them. I turned the pages and found my poem about the dragon pin:

> *The dragon is alone with his pretty ball.*
> *There is no one to play catch with.*
> *Hidden away in his cave,*
> *he waits for the light.*

And another, about the tree:

> *Do not mourn, little tree.*
> *Your brothers and sisters have been struck down—*
> *but you live still.*
> *Be strong!*
> *For you alone are the beginning*
> *of a whole new forest.*

I always looked forward to writing in my diary. It had become a great comfort to me—almost like a nightly meeting with a good friend.

Perhaps it could comfort me now. I could try to write about Tae-yul.

I held the pencil above a blank page.

———

Half an hour later I threw down the pencil in disgust. How many words had I written and crossed out?

My brother—older than me but still so young
You wear the wrong uniform—of a soldier, not a schoolboy
A short train ride over the mountain, but worlds away

It wasn't that the words were bad—they just weren't right. I couldn't understand it. I knew Tae-yul so well; why couldn't I write about him? And why was it different from writing about Uncle?

Maybe it was still too soon. I hadn't started writing about Uncle until weeks after he'd left. Tae-yul had been gone only a few hours. Perhaps when enough time had passed . . . Maybe this was the reason nothing I wrote satisfied me.

But I knew it wasn't the only reason.

I'd often been angry at Tae-yul, especially when he treated me like a baby. But just as often I'd looked at him and, without either of us saying a word, I'd known we were thinking the same thing. At those moments, his thoughts were my thoughts, my thoughts were his.

When he left, he took too many of my thoughts with him.

24. Tae-yul

About a dozen others are waiting at the station: young men like me, traveling to Seoul.

We all board the train. Most of the others put their bags on the floor. Not me—I hold mine on my lap. I want it close to me—my things from home.

Not much, really. A change of clothes. A lunch box. Somehow Omoni got some rice, just a handful, and all of it for me. Plus kimchee and beans. I can hardly believe I'll be eating rice again.

Sun-hee gave me a little envelope when I left the house. I open it on the train. Inside there's a piece of paper folded around a pressed flower. A rose of Sharon blossom. It's dried, so she must have had it for a while.

It was nice of her, but it worries me. Our bags will be inspected, for sure, either on the trip or once we arrive. Maybe the inspectors won't know what it is. But I can't risk that—can't risk anything that might make them send me home.

I could keep it in my pocket. But they'll probably take our clothes, too, when they give us uniforms.

I crumble the flower in my fist. Then I open my hand and blow the little pink pieces away.

It's OK, Sun-hee, I say to myself. *I don't need the flower. I'll remember without it.*

The training camp is outside Seoul. There are barracks, some other buildings, huge fields. We line up to register. We have to sign both our names—Japanese and Korean: Japanese because we're citizens of the Empire, Korean so they can keep track of us, of the ones who aren't really Japanese.

Haircut. Uniform. A kit bag for each of us with a second uniform inside. Everything gets done military style—no fussing, quick, efficient.

But there's still time to think. Like during the haircut. The Japanese had cut Grandfather's hair. Now they're cutting mine. The same thing so many years apart—but different. He was forced to have his hair cut. I've volunteered.

The kit bag is patched, like Sun-hee's clothes. My clothes

were patched, too, but it only bothered me to see hers, maybe because she's a girl. Girls care more about things like that.

The patches mean the bag was used before by another soldier.

For the first time I think about what it really means to be in the army. Whoever owned the bag before me might have been wounded and sent home. Or discharged for some other reason.

Or killed in the war. His kit bag reissued—to me.

A lucky kit bag? Or an unlucky one?

No use thinking of it as unlucky. I decide to think of it as my lucky kit bag.

We line up again outside the main building to listen to the camp's commanding officer. It's the usual speech about the divinity of the Emperor and the glory of his Empire. And a lot of stuff about discipline, hard work, the need for soldiers to be worthy of the Imperial uniform.

Finally, the commanding officer steps aside. One of the sergeants responsible for new recruits takes his place. "Your barracks is two kilometers away!" he barks. "You will go there now, running in lockstep! You will put away your gear in perfect order and report for dinner at exactly 1800 hours, back here at the mess hall! Dismissed!"

We all salute. The fellow next to me has a watch. "Eighteen hundred hours?" he mutters. "That's less than thirty minutes. We'd better get moving."

On our way we pass a lot of barracks. Soldiers are lined up outside, or else coming and going. Our barracks is the farthest away from the mess hall, the very last building. For the newest recruits.

The next few weeks are a blur. I'm always tired, so tired I can hardly think. Reveille at 0430 hours. Dress and straighten the barracks. Line up outside for roll call. Run to the mess hall. Breakfast, then our orders for the day.

We *still* attend classes every morning for an hour and a half. We have to study the Emperor's military code of honor, "The Imperial Rescript to Soldiers and Sailors," memorize it, and recite it back to the sergeants. There are other lessons, too. How to take apart a gun, clean it, put it back together. It's easy enough in the big room where we have our lessons, but then we have to do it outside. In the rain. In a muddy ditch. At night.

Lunch. The food isn't very good, but at least there's more than at home. Usually barley, a little dried fish, vegetables or pickles.

In the afternoon, we have physical training. Endless calisthenics. Running for hours with rocks in our kit bags. Uphill, always uphill. How can there be so much uphill with no downhill? Obstacle courses without our kit bags. Then the same again *with* the bags, and you have to try to beat your first time. If you don't, you have to run it again.

Back to the barracks. Clean up, put our stuff away, get ready for dinner. Run back to the mess hall. After dinner, sometimes more training. Or a lecture from the officers about military history and strategy. Trying hard to stay awake.

Back to the barracks for the last time. Laundry, the last duty of the day. Washing out that day's uniform, hanging it up to dry. Taking the other uniform, hung up the day before, brushing it, sewing loose buttons, darning any holes. Everything ready for the next morning.

And, finally, collapsing into bed. But not falling asleep—because most nights the sergeants roust us all out of bed again. To stand outside in nothing but our underwear and recite the Imperial Rescript—pages and pages long.

No use trying to fake it. The sergeants walk up and down our ranks, listening to each one of us: "The soldier and sailor should consider loyalty their paramount duty. . . . Remember always that duty is heavier than a mountain, while death is lighter than a feather. . . ." The whole thing takes about twenty minutes to recite.

For the first time in my life, I'm glad Abuji is a scholar—that I had his reputation to live up to. I never did, of course, but if I hadn't had to try, even a little, I wouldn't have been able to memorize this stuff.

If you mumble or try to skip over the parts you don't know, you're in trouble. One of the sergeants always carries a whip with him. The other keeps a club handy. One crack of the whip and your back is bleeding. One whack with the club and your buttocks turn to nothing but pain. Cry out or fall down and you get hit some more.

The first time this happens, it's a recruit behind me. He says the wrong words, or maybe he doesn't say the right ones loud enough. The whip cracks, we all stop reciting. The guy has fallen to his knees and the sergeant is coiling the whip for another lash. He sees us watching and his face goes purple.

"What are you doing?" he screams at us. "You want some of this, too?"

Immediately we face front and continue with the recitation. Behind me, I hear the whip crack again, and a cry like a dog's yelp. Another crack—another cry. *Shut up*, I'm begging the guy in my head. *Shut up. If you cry, he'll whip you again. . . .*

One more crack—and then silence. We're dismissed, and warned not to touch the guy. So we leave him as he is, curled up on the ground, a dark stain spreading on the back of his shirt.

We're punished for everything. The smallest things. We clean up the barracks, an ashtray isn't right in the middle of the table—somebody gets hit. We do calisthenics, and don't finish exactly together—somebody gets hit. Guys walk around with black eyes, gaps in their mouths from lost teeth, scars on their backs, bruises on their legs.

The Whipper tells us that the cruelty is necessary. That if we can put up with it, the ones who get through the training will be tough enough for anything the enemy does.

Not everybody makes it through. In the first month, four get sent home in disgrace. Their lives worthless now—back home the Japanese will treat them like garbage. A shame to themselves and worse, to their families.

Not me. I'm not going home that way. Uncle would have made it through this and I will too. I think about the two soldiers who took my bicycle. The officer who had Sun-hee's diary burned. The one who wanted my help to trap Uncle, the faceless ones who beat him up, the others who might be hunting him down even now.

I'll never let them win.

25. Sun-hee

A few days after Tae-yul's departure a Japanese soldier came to the house and delivered small sacks of rice and dried fish.

"For the family of the brave young man who volunteered his services to His Divine Majesty!" he announced as he presented the sacks to Abuji. Abuji bent his head down in a partial bow. The soldier saluted and left.

Abuji took the sacks to the kitchen and handed them to Omoni. I went to help her put them away.

I found a wooden box to store them in. When I turned toward her, I saw Omoni holding the sacks away from her, as if they contained something nasty. The expression on her face was like a bitter wind.

I could guess what she was thinking. Ten thousand bags of rice and fish wouldn't have made up for Tae-yul's absence. "Omoni," I said gently, "Tae-yul is proud of what he's doing for us. We must prepare and eat this food with gladness in our hearts."

Omoni looked at me for a moment, then back at the bags in her hands. Her face softened; she put the bags down hastily and wiped away a tear. "You are right, Sun-hee. Here is what we will do—we will prepare a little celebration meal with this food. I think that would please Tae-yul."

She smiled at me. But only her lips smiled, not her eyes.

Four weeks after Tae-yul left, Abuji walked into the courtyard. He seemed to be standing a little straighter, and looked as cheerful as I'd ever seen him. I knew the reason right away. Only one thing could make us feel all at once as if it were a holiday: a letter from Tae-yul.

Abuji read it aloud to us.

Dear family,

I wish I could have written sooner, but you would hardly believe how busy our days are. We rise very early and straighten the barracks for inspection. Then we have breakfast, followed

132

by several hours of study. And I thought that being out of school would mean no more books for me! On the contrary, we have many things to learn. There are procedures and operations, of course, for our mission. In addition, we spend a lot of time reading the Emperor's words for inspiration and guidance. We memorize his speeches and recite them to our commanding officers.

In the afternoon we have physical training. It is very challenging at times, and of course the sergeant demands our every effort. On many occasions we train without the necessary equipment, to simulate a crisis that might actually happen in battle.

We are fortunate that we continue to receive the supplies necessary for our training sessions. Food is plentiful, if somewhat limited in variety. They have given us two uniforms each. Omoni, you would be surprised to hear that our duties include keeping our uniforms in top condition. Our uniforms are inspected often, so I am an expert at laundry now. We do our laundry every evening. Then we study some more and sleep very gratefully!

I hope this letter finds you all in good health. Please do not worry about me, for I am doing fine. I think of you all often, always with love and respect.

> *With deepest affection,*
> *Your son and brother*

Letter writing required a very formal style, quite different from the way Tae-yul spoke. The letter didn't really sound like him, but it was enough to know he'd written those very words.

Abuji read it to us again. When he finished the second time, Omoni clasped her hands and spoke, her eyes shining.

"He sounds very well! My, they train them a long time, don't they?"

I knew why she sounded so happy. If Tae-yul was still training, then he hadn't yet been sent to the battlefront. He was safe.

I couldn't wait to read the letter for myself—to see if there was anything in it for me to figure out. "Abuji, may I have the letter for now? To read again?"

He nodded, folded the letter carefully back into its envelope, and handed it to me. I took it and went out into the garden.

I read through the letter quickly first, then went back to the beginning. "*In addition, we spend a lot of time reading the Emperor's words for inspiration and guidance. We memorize his speeches and recite them to our commanding officers.*" I almost laughed out loud. Here indeed was a place where Tae-yul had left invisible traces of his true feelings on the page. As a student, he'd always hated learning the Emperor's words! I could almost hear him now: "*Isn't that one of the silliest things you have ever heard? Imagine making soldiers spend time memorizing speeches instead of preparing for battle!*"

There were several more lines in which Tae-yul seemed to be saying more than his actual words.

"*The sergeant demands our every effort.*" I could well imagine that. A Japanese sergeant, yelling at the recruits every minute. I hoped he wasn't too hard on Tae-yul.

"*. . . fortunate that we continue to receive supplies . . .*" I was surprised that this line had escaped the censors' attention. It implied strongly that supplies were low—so low that Tae-yul was grateful for them, when really they should be something he took for granted. The food, too—"*limited in variety.*"

Surely, the army ought to be receiving the best of food. At least that's what the Japanese had been telling us for years—that our rice was needed by the army. And what about training *"without the necessary equipment?"* Was this really to make them practice for a battle crisis? Or because the equipment wasn't available?

"... laundry ... study some more ... sleep very gratefully!" That had to be another way of saying that he was thoroughly exhausted. Tae-yul had never done laundry in his life before this. How tedious it must be at the end of a long day to have to worry about preparing his uniform for the next day's inspection.

And I was sure that the last paragraph contained his thoughts clear and undisguised. Including the way he'd signed it, without using his name. For he'd have had to use his Japanese name—Kaneyama Nobuo, instead of Kim Tae-yul.

All in all, the letter seemed quite critical of the military. Most of the supplies and equipment must be going to the war itself, so there was little to spare for training new recruits. I thought about it for a while and finally decided that Tae-yul was trying to say that the war was still going badly for the Japanese.

Even beyond the pleasure of getting the letter, there was double joy in it for me: the satisfaction of figuring out Tae-yul's real message and the good news it carried.

We prepared a box to send to Tae-yul. Omoni put in a little pot of bean paste and a paper packet of *go-kam,* his favorite sweet of dried persimmons.

Mrs. Ahn had a persimmon tree in her garden. In the fall it was truly magnificent: The leaves fell and left the branches

135

bare except for the brilliant orange fruits. The soldiers came every year and took most of the persimmons away, but she always managed to hide some. She dried them until they were the size of little plums and stored them all through the winter. Sometimes when we did errands for her she would give me one. I always sucked it instead of chewing, to keep its sweet golden taste in my mouth as long as I could.

I had never known Omoni to ask Mrs. Ahn for anything before, but she did now. She asked for two persimmons to send to Tae-yul. Mrs. Ahn didn't even nod; she went right into her house and came back with a handful—at least a dozen of them, probably all she had left. It made my mouth water just to look at them.

I could have asked Omoni for one. She'd have given it to me; she knew I loved *go-kam* as much as Tae-yul did. But it didn't seem right to want a piece when he was in the army so far from home.

And as I wrapped the dried fruit carefully, I wished we were making another box as well—for Uncle.

We all wrote letters to send with the box. Abuji and I wrote our own, then I wrote one for Omoni—she told me what to say. She put in a scarf she'd made, too. She'd started it right after Tae-yul left, unraveling two old pairs of mittens to get the yarn. Blue and black, knitted together. It wasn't very pretty, but it would be warm. The spring nights were still chilly, but I thought Omoni would have sent the scarf no matter what the weather—just to have something to send.

When everything was in the box, Abuji sealed it and took it to the post office. The mail wasn't very reliable these days, but surely they'd be more careful with something sent to a soldier. At least we hoped so. I felt pleased when I went to bed that night, imagining Tae-yul opening the box and finding all those nice things.

26. Tae-yul

At the end of the third week we're allowed to write letters home. We have to put them into the envelopes unsealed—the censors will read them first. I try to make mine cheerful, because I don't want anyone at home to worry about me. Especially Omoni. Besides, I'm doing fine.

I'm in better shape than most of the others. All that work building the airstrip—I've gotten pretty strong. The physical training is always tough, but I get through it. Some of the guys puke or collapse and can't finish. And then they get beaten by the sergeant and have to do the worst jobs around camp.

I keep my mouth shut except for yes, sir—no, sir—right away, sir. I get things done when they need to be done. The sergeant and the other officers leave me alone. It's sort of like acting again—acting like a good soldier.

But sometimes at night I have trouble falling asleep, even though I'm exhausted. Because I'm not sure if I can keep the act going once I'm in combat. In combat a good soldier doesn't just get up the hill first. Or load his gun fastest.

In combat a good soldier kills people. Americans—the ones who are trying to free Korea.

I know it will come sooner or later—the time when I won't be able to act anymore. But I don't know when. Or what I'll do.

End of the sixth week of training. Only two weeks to go. A box from home arrives with letters from everyone and a scarf. There's a crumpled paper packet, too—empty but sticky. I sniff at it. *Go-kam*. Somehow Omoni got some for me. But it's gone, stolen somewhere along the way. None of us soldiers ever get any of the food we're sent.

The letters cheer me up. Omoni tells me to keep warm, to fold a newspaper and put it under my shirt to keep out the wind; wear the scarf always, even in bed; drink a lot of soup. Mother stuff. Odd how I can hear her voice, even in Sun-hee's handwriting.

Sun-hee's own letter is a funny one. It describes Spade-face getting splashed with mud when a car drove by. Of course she doesn't say Spade-face. She says, "the man who walks down our street often," and I know who she means. Spade-face, always so proud of his uniform.

She also tells about getting rice and fish from the Japanese. I'm glad to know that—it's doing them a little good, my being in the army. Sun-hee says to write again soon, that she enjoys reading my letter over and over. I know that's her way of saying she's tried to figure out what I really meant. Her letter ends by telling me that my handwriting isn't too terrible, she gives it a passing grade. I laugh out loud.

Abuji's letter is more like a note. Short, saying everything is fine at home. He thanks me for the food, as if I've given it to him myself. He finishes by saying he's looking forward to having a long talk with me one day about my experience in the army.

I'm surprised by the lump in my throat.

Week seven.

The officers eat in a separate room and are served by soldiers. It's my unit's week to provide servers. Me and two others. One more duty, added to all the rest. Our classes and training are cut short by thirty minutes so we can rush to the mess hall. When the officers are done eating, we're allowed to eat. By that time everyone else is nearly finished; we have to wolf down our food so we can get to the next duty on time.

The officers always talk like the servers aren't there. Or at least like we can't hear. That's fine with us—it's even useful sometimes. The servers learn things. Like: rifle inspection the next day. Back at the barracks, the servers tell everyone so we can get our guns in order.

I move around the tables as quietly as I can. It makes me think of Sun-hee—how she used to listen in when she cleared the table at home. I smile a little. She might have fooled Abuji and Uncle sometimes, but I always knew what she was doing.

I carry in a bowl of rice. The commanding officer is talking. "Ridiculous even to ask us," he says angrily. He's in a bad mood about something. "They forget that we are training *Koreans* here."

I don't like the way he says it. Like we're a breed of dog—a stupid breed.

"There isn't a single soldier here who would volunteer for such a mission," the CO goes on. "How do they expect me to submit five names? It comes down to this: Either I send them five unwilling soldiers, or else I tell them I don't have any at all."

"They must not be unwilling," another officer objects. "It would be a serious mistake to send any who are. It is too great a responsibility."

"My point exactly," snaps the CO. "Oh, they're fine as foot

soldiers—they can slog through the mud as well as anyone. But for something like this? Can you imagine any Korean brave enough?"

He's calling us cowards! But not to our faces. He just assumes we're not brave enough for—for whatever it is—without even asking.

The rest of that evening, the whole night, his words rub against my mind like a blister getting sorer and sorer. I hardly sleep. By morning I know I have to do something.

Morning roll call. Sure enough, it's something special. All the officers are there, not just the sergeant.

The sergeant announces an extraordinary assignment. So demanding, requiring such bravery, that no one will be ordered to accept it. Volunteers only. And no guarantee that a volunteer will qualify. The assignment is that tough.

I don't think anymore. I click my heels and snap off a salute. "Sir!" I almost shout. I'm looking straight ahead in perfect position. I can't see anyone's face. But later when the other soldiers talk about it, they tell me the officers' mouths all dropped clean open.

The sergeant says, "Kaneyama! Are you volunteering? Do you understand that this mission may require the ultimate sacrifice from you?"

"Yes, sir. This soldier is brave enough, sir. For any job or mission. Sir!"

I stand there at attention. I can feel the surprise in the air, even though no one says anything. I can tell by the way they're shifting about.

After I say that, three others volunteer. The sergeant dismisses everyone but us. "Report to the CO's office," he says. "Briefing on your new assignment. You'll be shipping out to Japan in two days."

Two days! So soon?

The four of us salute, then march together to our briefing.

27. Sun-hee

The cherry trees blossomed all over town. A few days later the ground looked as if it were covered with pale pink snow as the petals fell and were carried by the wind everywhere. Our rose of Sharon tree grew new leaves, too. There were only a few shoots. But it had survived another winter, and Omoni and I were delighted.

In May we got Tae-yul's second letter—weeks after he'd written it. Abuji said we were lucky to receive it; the war had all but stopped regular mail service.

Dear family,

I am sure it will be a surprise to you to hear that after only a few weeks of training, I am being sent to Japan. I can assure you it was just as big a surprise to me! A few of us have been recruited for a special assignment, by order of the Emperor. I was chosen because of my previous commitment to the Youth Air Corps. We are to be transported to a new base in Japan. You must understand that I cannot tell you the exact location. We will have further training for our new positions. Please do not worry about me. As always, I will do my utmost to make the whole family proud of me.

Your son and brother

Once again, Omoni was happy to hear that Tae-yul was still in training. For my part, I wondered why the letter was so short. It seemed quite straightforward, without any hidden meaning. Probably he had written it in a hurry and

141

hadn't had time to put in a message for me to figure out.

One evening a few days later I couldn't write in my diary because my pencil had worn down to nothing but a stub. Abuji would have to bring me another one from his school. It annoyed me to miss a day in my diary.

I was in Uncle and Tae-yul's room. I'd taken to using it as kind of a study; I didn't want them to come home to a room with the stale, musty feel of having been empty for a long time.

I put my diary back on the shelf and took both of Tae-yul's letters from the box where I kept them. I loved reading them over and over. I loved knowing that my brother had touched the sheets of paper I was holding.

For the hundredth time I wished we'd gotten more letters. Abuji had said they'd probably allow him to write us before he was shipped out for combat, and Omoni held on tightly to that idea. It was good *not* to get a letter from him, she said, because that meant he was safe. Another way the war turned everything inside out.

I refolded the first letter, put it carefully back in the box, and studied the second letter yet again. I was curious about Tae-yul's new assignment. There didn't seem to be any clues, but maybe I'd missed something. . . .

"A few of us have been recruited for a special assignment, by order of the Emperor. I was chosen because of my previous commitment to the Youth Air Corps."

"By order of the Emperor"? It seemed strange that he'd write this phrase in a letter. It made him sound like the announcer on Radio Tokyo or the block leader at a neighborhood accounting. Did he mean to sound like that? Why? To remind me of something? What?

142

". . . *my previous commitment to the Youth Air Corps.*" I thought back to those days—not really so long ago, but it felt like years. What had he done when he was in the Youth Air Corps?

The airstrip. Digging with spades all day long.

Perhaps he was being assigned to dig trenches. I didn't know much about war, and hardly anything about battles, but I guessed that trenches would probably be dug quite near the front line. I hoped that wasn't Tae-yul's new assignment. Then again, digging trenches was surely better than being sent to the front line itself?

By order of the Emperor. The Youth Air Corps.

Emperor . . . Air . . .

Tae-yul was going to be a kamikaze.

He was going to fly an airplane for that unit—the Special Attack Unit. How often I'd heard him use those words! That was the reason for the extra training. Surely, pilots needed a lot of training.

And after the training—a mission.

A suicide mission.

I was so frightened by this idea that I could no longer sit still. I stood and paced around the room.

It was crazy. *I* was crazy. I had to be wrong. I was imagining things—those words might mean something completely different.

No—I was right. It was so like Tae-yul to want to fly an airplane. Maybe he thought that if he was going to die anyway, it might as well happen when he was doing something he wanted to do.

But maybe I was wrong. *Remember Tomo—remember*

Uncle. I'd been so sure, and had made a terrible mistake. *Don't make a mistake this time.*

I slipped into the other bedroom and got into bed without either of my parents noticing. If they'd seen me or talked to me, they'd have known something was wrong. I didn't even have to look in the mirror to know that my face was pale and strained.

In bed I lay flat on my back, forcing myself to think. *The war is going badly for the Japanese. Tae-yul said so—there are rumors in the street . . . and the lessons at school—no news of victories anywhere, not for a long time now. If he's going to be a kamikaze, he'll need a lot of training. The war is almost over— how much longer? Maybe it will end before he gets to fly a mission. . . .*

That was it. That was the answer. If somehow Tae-yul could be stopped, or at least delayed, for a month perhaps— even a week or two might be long enough.

But how?

The next day at school we had bayonet practice and bomb drills, but I was so inattentive and listless that the teacher thought I was ill. She sent me home early in the afternoon.

When I walked into the courtyard, Omoni dropped the wet laundry she was holding and rushed over to me. "Sun-hee! What's the matter—are you all right? Has something happened?"

I shook my head. "I'm fine, Omoni. Just tired. But the teacher thought I shouldn't work anymore."

She put her hand on my cheek and made me open my mouth so she could look at my throat. "Go to bed," she said. "I'll bring you some soup."

I felt a little guilty going to bed; after all, I wasn't really sick. I should have helped Omoni with the laundry. But I needed the quiet time alone, to think.

After I'd drunk the soup Omoni brought me—it wasn't really soup, just the water the vegetables had been boiled in, but we always called it soup—I lay quietly on my mat and waited. When it was nearly time for Abuji to come home, I got up, rolled my sleeping mat, and put it away. Then I combed my hair. I arranged two cushions on the floor. Finally, I went to Tae-yul's room and fetched both letters.

I sat down on one of the cushions and waited. After a few minutes I heard Abuji come into the house. I heard him speak briefly with Omoni. Then he came into the bedroom. "Sun-hee—you are not in bed?" he said. "I hope this means you are feeling better."

"Yes, Abuji. I'm fine, thank you. Would you sit with me for a few minutes? I have something I would like to talk to you about."

He slid the door shut and sat down on the other cushion. "Please go ahead," he said.

I hesitated for a moment. Tae-yul might not approve of what I was about to do. But he'd never said not to tell anyone what I discovered in his letters. Maybe, in a way, he wanted us to know, all of us.

I took a deep breath and let it out slowly. The last of my uncertainty was blown away with that breath.

"Abuji, before he left, Tae-yul told me he wouldn't be able to write his true thoughts in his letters—because they'd be censored. He asked me to read his words carefully, so I would be able to figure out what he *really* meant."

Abuji looked thoughtful. "So you believe his letters have

145

messages of importance beyond the actual words?" he asked.

I smiled a little inside. Abuji was making things easier for me. "Yes. The second one especially. I do not know if it's a message he intended to put in, or if it was almost . . . accidental on his part. But last night I understood the letter in a different way."

It took me a while to explain everything. I had to go back in time, to talk about how fascinated Tae-yul had always been by the kamikaze. Then I showed Abuji the first letter, and pointed out the places where I'd uncovered Tae-yul's true thoughts.

Finally, I unfolded the second letter and held it out to him. I no longer needed to look at it myself; I'd memorized the whole thing. After he read through it quickly, I revealed my true fear: That Tae-yul's new assignment was kamikaze training.

Abuji never once interrupted me. He listened intently to every word. He didn't shake his head or act like I was crazy. I was grateful for that.

When I finished, we sat in silence for a few moments. Abuji drew in a long breath and let it out slowly, just as I had before I started talking. Then he said, "Is it your wish that I act on what you have told me? That I do something to prevent your brother from taking part in a mission?"

"Abuji, the war may end soon. I thought that if Tae-yul could be delayed—even for a little while—perhaps there would be no need for him to fly a mission at all."

Abuji nodded thoughtfully. "Let us say, for the moment, that you are correct about your brother," he said evenly. "Suppose I went to the military authorities. What could I say to them that might have the desired result?"

I was ready with an answer to that; it was what I'd been thinking about all day. Still, I spoke slowly, looking down at my hands. "At first I thought perhaps you could say that he had some illness—some kind of medical condition that would be bad for a pilot. But I don't think that would work. He has already been training for so long—they would know by now that there is nothing wrong with him." I paused.

Abuji nodded again, so I went on. "But what if—what if you were to tell them something like the truth? Tell them that Uncle is a resistance worker—they know that already, right? And that Tae-yul admired Uncle greatly. And therefore you think Tae-yul should not be trusted on a mission of such importance. He should be stopped from flying."

I'd turned this plan over in my mind a hundred times. It would not be betraying Uncle. I was not asking Abuji to tell a bald-faced lie. And it might save Tae-yul's life.

Abuji was quiet for what seemed like a long time. As I waited for him to speak, I suddenly felt exhausted. The sleepless night and restless day of thinking so hard and now telling my thoughts had left my body limp. At that moment I didn't think I could even lift my hand.

At last Abuji spoke in his usual calm, even voice. "Well, then. I could tell the authorities I believe Tae-yul is not to be trusted. What do you think they would do?"

Something in his face made my stomach feel a little queasy. "They wouldn't want someone like that flying one of their planes, so they—they would stop him. Wouldn't they, Abuji?"

Abuji nodded. "And then what?"

I stared at him with my mouth open. It wasn't very polite of me, but I was too surprised to control my expression. How could I not have thought of this myself?

Abuji answered his own question. "They would arrest him. If he were lucky, he would be imprisoned. Otherwise . . ."

He didn't need to finish the sentence. I closed my eyes as a terrible fear rose in me.

Otherwise, the Japanese would execute him as a traitor.

If Tae-yul were not stopped, he would crash his plane and die. If he *were* stopped, he might die before a firing squad.

Abuji raised his hands and rubbed his eyes as if he, too, were very tired. He spoke with his hands still covering his face. "Sun-hee, I am deeply grateful to you for speaking to me about this. I must think about it for a while. I will tell you when I make a decision."

He lowered his hands. "Now, if you are feeling well enough, perhaps you could help your mother with dinner."

I rose from my seat and went to the door. Before I stepped out I looked back at him. He was sitting with his hands in his lap, head bowed, shoulders slumped.

I closed the door behind me and stood there for a moment, trembling.

I had never before seen Abuji look afraid.

The next day after school, I waited outside the house for Abuji to come home. I wanted to talk to him before he came inside, because I didn't know whether he'd told Omoni anything and I had a million questions to ask. Had he gone to the authorities? What had he said to them? What did they say in response? Would Tae-yul be coming home soon?

But when he came home, all the questions died in my throat. He looked at me and nodded, his face tired and gentle. Then he shook his head and took me by the hand, so we went inside together.

Without a word he'd told me what I needed to know. He had given them the information. But he had no idea what they'd do next.

We could only wait.

28. *Tae-yul*

The last night before I leave for Japan. I'm wide awake on my bunk. Somewhere in the middle of the darkness it finally sinks in.

I've volunteered for the Special Attack Unit—the kamikaze.

That's the new assignment. Mine and two other soldiers'. They've chosen three of us, dismissed the fourth with no explanation.

All through the briefing, the CO droning on and on about duty and honor and courage, and I hardly heard him. There was only one thought in my head.

I'm going to fly an airplane!

That was the only thing I'd thought about. Until now.

Now the whole truth looms over me. I'm going to fly an airplane—and *crash it.* Into an American ship. It grabs me by the shoulders and sits me straight up in bed, that's how strong it is. Impossible! How can anyone do something like that?

I joined the army to save Uncle. Not for any other reason. Not to kill Americans. And *certainly* not to help the Japanese.

But that's what the Imperial forces do—the Special Attack Unit most of all. It's not just the damage they do to American ships. It's the power they have to boost the whole army. They make everyone, even lowly guards like Spade-face, believe in the Japanese cause. He said it himself: As long as there are those willing to become kamikaze, there's no way Japan can lose.

How did I get here? How can I be part of that?

A sudden sound in my head—a grinding noise. It takes me a second to realize it's me, grinding my teeth. My hands are clenched in fists, too—I want to hit something.

I've given my word. If I back out now, they'll think they were right, that Koreans *are* cowards. I'd lose face completely and never get it back.

And besides—it sounds stupid, selfish, but I *want* to fly an airplane.

There has to be a way. To fly, but not to help them.

My jaw relaxes a little. I lie back on my bunk, staring at the ceiling. I spend the rest of the night digging through my mind for everything I've ever heard about the kamikaze.

Gray light at the window. And I have a plan.

Now everything is happening in such a rush. There's no time to think. Packing, saying goodbye to the fellows in my unit. We got to be friends really fast here. The guy in the next bunk, Han-joo—Kentaro is his Japanese name—salutes me. Everyone laughs, but it still makes me feel funny. We're the same rank. But he knows—we all know—as soon as you become a pilot, you're automatically made an officer.

Leaving Korea, going to Japan. My first time on the open sea.

A lot of the other guys on the boat get sick. I don't, even though my stomach feels awful the whole time. Flying in a plane probably won't feel like being on a boat. But maybe a plane rides up and down on the air, like the boat on the waves. I practice breathing deep, trying to control the sloshing in my stomach. Just in case it feels the same.

My new camp is not far from Tokyo, at a base called Kagohara. The barracks are a lot nicer. There's a platform for sleeping on, with mattresses, not straw mats. And only six men to a room. New uniforms, too.

But the same morning routine. Lessons on the Emperor's words, reciting the Rescript. Pages and pages to memorize. What does any of it have to do with flying?

We get other lessons on the workings of airplanes. We don't have to prepare them for flight, or fix them if they break down—mechanics do that. But a pilot has to know his plane as well as he knows his own body. Better, even. If anything goes wrong in the air, there are things a pilot can do to compensate. But only if he knows exactly what's wrong.

I love these classes, learning about the engines. It's funny when I think about it, my education in machines. From bicycle right to airplane, nothing in between. Well, maybe one thing—Uncle's printing press.

When we go out to the hangars to see the engines for ourselves, I notice that the pilots ignore the mechanics. They're considered a lower class, not just by military rank. I feel bad for them. I wouldn't mind being a mechanic myself, getting to work with engines all the time. And I'm impressed by how well they know the planes.

More lessons: flight manuals, military operations, military history. We try to learn everything. It's impossible, but we try anyway. Every free moment back at the barracks we go around carrying books and manuals.

Even in the latrine. If you have to wait to use it, you can hear the guy inside reciting a lesson. Uncle would have made a good joke about that. And I'd have laughed, except that I'm doing it, too.

In the afternoons we have "practical training." Flying at last!

But not in planes—in gliders. We watch the other squads. The glider is attached to a car with a long cable. The car tows the glider until it gets up enough speed, then the pilot releases the cable. When our instructors demonstrate, the glider banks in a gentle curve and then rises in a big spiral. It's beautiful to watch.

But when it's the new recruits piloting, ha!—a whole different story. The glider crawls along the ground, wobbling back and forth, sometimes lifting a meter or two into the air. Sun-hee has a swing in a tree back home. She gets higher on that than they do in the gliders.

Our instructors say that when the whole squad can fly gliders properly, we'll move on to planes. If we're good at it, we could be flying planes next month.

My first time in the glider. The instructor sits behind me. First he flies it, telling me the whole time what he's doing. The control is a stick that raises or lowers the nose. It directs the wings, too. I listen hard, so I can't really look to see how high we are. I know from watching the others that he'll take it up to about five meters. Then he'll bring it back down again, for me to try.

My turn. The car gains speed. The instructor yells, "Now!" and I push the button to release the cable.

The glider slithers along on its belly like a snake. Push the stick, pull it precisely, at just the right moment—and we're off the ground!

The glider stays in the air for a few seconds. It feels like a few *years*. Magic, that's the only word for it. Then it bumps down again, tipping a little on the landing so the instructor has to help me straighten it.

I wish he hadn't had to help, but still I'm proud of myself—some of the other guys can't even get the glider up at all. It rolls along and careens in crazy S patterns when they panic and start pushing the stick every which way.

I can't wait to fly a real plane. There are only two planes for the whole camp, more than two hundred men. So even when we do start to fly, we'll have to take turns.

Still, it's a thrill to see them for the first time.

They're kept in the forest at the edge of camp, hidden under pine boughs in case of an enemy air raid. The planes used to be kept in hangars, but the huge buildings are easy to spot from the air. So all the training planes were moved to the woods.

It's one of the duties of new recruits to jog out to the woods and uncover the planes. The feel and smell of pine again.

Ai, they're beautiful! So slim. The cockpit is the widest part—just wide enough to hold a man or two men, one sitting behind the other. Then the plane tapers down to the tail. The propeller blades are enormous—three of them, each as tall as me. What power! And the wings are broad and flat, like two strong arms.

We uncover the planes after lunch and cover them up again at the end of the day. That's the closest we get to them for weeks.

I can see why it's organized like that. Being so close to the planes every day, but not able to fly them, makes us want to do even better at our training. So we'll be able to fly soon.

Our squad makes progress. Thirty of us—three Koreans, the rest Japanese. Our instructors are very pleased—they say we're all fast learners, considering we don't get many chances to fly the gliders.

We're flying more often than they know. The controls for the rudder are foot pedals. After lights out we sit on our beds, imaginary stick in front of us, imaginary pedals on the floor, our hands and feet moving, every one of us flying a glider in our minds.

The day finally arrives—our first day in the planes! Reveille at 0430. The morning lesson on the Emperor's sayings is agony. Then after lunch we have to endure another speech. When the CO starts talking, I feel like I'll die from impatience.

But this speech is different from the others. For the first time ever the CO is saying something different about the war.

Losing—Japan is losing. He doesn't use that word, but for nearly an hour he talks about recent battles. The numbers of casualties—men, planes, equipment . . . The never-ending waves of U.S. planes, the strength of the American naval fleet . . . How the Japanese have been forced to fall back, and back, and back . . . How they've lost nearly all the territory they conquered earlier in the war.

And how the battle in the air is Japan's last hope.

"Our sacred homeland now lies under direct threat of American bombardment," he says. "The responsibility for any chance of an honorable end to this war rests on our pilots—on you, should you complete your training successfully. You must all apply yourselves with utmost diligence and not waste a single moment of your instruction. In the name of the Emperor!" He dismisses us with a fervent salute.

154

The squad is quiet after hearing all that. But then our instructors yell for us to march. Double time to the airstrip, where the planes are waiting for us, uncovered by the new recruits.

We aren't new anymore. We're ready to fly.

I talk to myself all the way out to the airstrip. *You've wanted so badly to fly. This is bound to be a letdown. It'll be different somehow—not nearly as good as you've imagined. Expect that and you won't be disappointed.*

Me in the front seat now, with the instructor behind. We have radio headsets! They're wonderful—it's like his voice is inside my head. Except I keep forgetting to press the button down when I want to talk. It's embarrassing—I answer him, then he repeats the question. And then I realize that I haven't pressed the button.

Headset. Harness. I feel the rudder pedals with my feet—bigger and heavier than the ones in the glider.

The plane starts to roll. I hear the instructor's voice the whole time. I try to listen hard. Throttle forward, accelerate—I really *am* listening. But only with part of my brain.

The rest of it is looking out the cockpit windshield. At the ground, sliding faster and faster beneath us. And then I can feel it, I can tell the exact moment that the wheels leave the ground. We're in the air!

The noise is incredible. At first I can hardly hear myself think. But then we're climbing—climbing fast! Noise—and the power to go with it.

In no time we're high above the airfield. The instructor banks the plane—his voice is in my head—something about going easy on the control . . .

I can't listen anymore. I have to look down at the ground.

Everything is so tiny! The trees are like little sprouts, the buildings like toys.

The seat is beneath me, I know that, and then the under-carriage of the plane, and the wheels.

But all I feel underneath me is air.

I was wrong. It's *better* than I imagined. I want to shout, as loud as I can. But of course that wouldn't be very soldierly. I might even get in trouble.

So I shout silently—one enormous yell of joy.

More flying lessons. I pilot the plane several times, with the instructor in the second seat—two sets of controls, in case of trouble. If you go out three times in a row without him having to touch his controls, you get to solo.

I'm one of the first. Flying feels so natural. Timing, control, speed—like playing with my top when I was little. Or riding my bike. I feel like I was born to do this.

We have so many things to learn. How to take off with as little runway as possible. How to control the plane no matter what the weather. How to land properly—very important, as even a small mistake on landing can damage the plane.

After we solo for a while, the instructor rides in the plane again. Now he demonstrates all kinds of maneuvers and teaches us to fly them. Then he gives us a series of tests: He puts the plane into a dive, and we have to climb out of it. Or he makes the plane spin, forcing us to regain control. With the plane upside down, he cuts the power. We have to get the power back on and get the plane right side up again.

Still more to learn: another plane in the air, pretending to be the enemy, so we can practice evasive maneuvers. Some-times scary, always exciting.

The time comes for us to practice our actual mission tactics. There's no way to do this, really. Two different tactics. The dive approach: target, the radio tower. We go into a dive from high above. But of course we have to pull up and out well above the target.

There's also the wave-hopping approach. For this we fly in low, as if we're just above the waves but beneath enemy fire, in a straight line toward the target "ship"—a marked tree on the edge of the field. Again, we pull out and up before we hit the tree.

The first few times we try the dive approach, we all pull out too soon. Hundreds of meters from the tower. It looks so foolish, watching the others from the ground. But when you're the pilot, it feels like the tower is right up your nose.

Our instructors are disgusted with us, they make us run around the airfield, stifling in our heavy canvas jumpsuits, until most of us have collapsed. Like little ants crawling around the perimeter of the field.

When we finally get so we're pulling out only fifty meters or so from the tower, they give us our next assignment: Do the dive *with our eyes closed*. This is to practice the timing, to prove that we know the planes and our flying abilities so well that we can tell where we are without looking.

The first time, I open my eyes at least half a dozen times. Impossible, what they're asking us to do—I feel like I'm going to crash right into the tower. But it's funny, how—how *interested* I feel. I like it, the challenge of it—I want to prove I can do it. Not to them. To myself.

They had us count during our earlier dives, so we know about how long it will take before we have to pull out: ten seconds from two thousand meters. The second try with my eyes closed, I start counting. How far could I get without

157

looking? *One. Two. Three—don't peek, get to five.* I try to picture the tower, getting bigger and bigger . . . *Four. Five—don't peek, get to seven . . .*

I can feel the sweat pouring down my face and body. I yell at myself inside my head—*Don't look!*—and squeeze my eyes shut tighter. Those last few seconds are the longest in my whole life.

At ten I open my eyes, blink once to clear them. The tower, right where I thought it would be. I pull out and go soaring.

That day I don't have to run.

Reveille one morning in June. The sergeant shouts for full dress uniforms. We've only worn them twice—on our first day here, then again when we got to fly the planes for the first time.

We line up. I take a quick glance around. In our uniforms we're a pretty smart-looking bunch. The CO seems to think so, too. He praises us for our success in training.

Then he assigns us our mission date.

Four days: If the weather's clear, we leave in four days.

For Operation "Kikusui," off Japan.

"Your assignments are posted on the barracks," he says. Then he turns to the sergeant, who explains how the assignments work. The best students have been assigned as fighters or bombers. Then signalmen, and last, mechanics.

Not one of us moves—we all remain standing at attention—but I can feel the shock go through my body and I'm sure the other trainees are feeling the same. Signalmen? Mechanics? That means *some of us won't be flying*.

What if I'm assigned mechanic? A few short weeks ago

I thought I wouldn't mind having that job. But those mechanics—they trained as pilots, too. Now they work on planes all the time and never have a chance to fly one. I'd hate that.

Then a thought hits me so hard I feel my stomach lurch. My plan! For my plan to work, I *have* to be a pilot. If I get the wrong assignment . . . if I can't fly . . .

We're dismissed, and there's a mad rush to the barracks. Everyone crowds around the assignment sheet posted on the wall. I get bumped and jostled and have to wait forever for my turn. I'm praying silently, *please, please* . . .

Running my eyes down the list. The K names.

KANEYAMA Nobuo. *Bomber.*

None of us is truly ready to fly a mission, but the military command is desperate. No squad is getting full training. We've been luckier than some—we've had target practice for more than a month now.

We don't get bream for our last meal. They must not have any. We get rice and beans, but instead of bream some kind of meat. It's been a long time since I've had any meat. This stuff is tough and full of gristle. I don't even want to know what it is.

Back to the barracks one last time. Each of us is given a little box for our things. We trim our nails and put the trimmings in a little envelope. A lock of hair, too. Both Koreans and Japanese do this, something about leaving behind whatever you can that your parents have given you.

Then we write letters home. I don't know what to say at first. But once I start writing, it gets easier. When I reach the end, I hesitate for a moment. They've promised us that these

159

won't be censored, that no one but our families will read them. I don't know if I believe that or not. But it will be my last letter ever, so I sign it with my real name.

The excitement has been washed away by a huge wave of fear—so strong that I feel the blood drain from my face. But it's too hard to imagine that the day after tomorrow I won't be here on this earth. It's probably better that way.

I put the letter on top of the box. Then I lie around on my bunk for the rest of the night. I don't think any of us sleep. I know I don't, anyway. I think about home. Not about Omoni—it makes me too sad. Or about Abuji either—it's uncomfortable, somehow, thinking about him. Mostly I think about Sun-hee and Uncle.

Sun-hee. She's a nice kid, even with all those questions. One good thing about never getting back home, I joke to myself—I won't have to answer a million questions. And Uncle. Best of all, thinking about Uncle. It makes me feel less sad to know that he'd be proud of me . . . if he knew. He won't know, of course—there's no way to ever tell him. But I feel like he'll know somehow. Not know it as a fact, but feel it in his heart. He'll think the best of me, anyway.

Then I think about other things. Girls. I've never had a girlfriend. Hee-won, Jung-shin's older sister—I wish I could have gotten to know her better. Maybe we could have talked about things, about her family being *chin-il-pa*, about me joining the army, how life gets so complicated sometimes.

Now the simplest things seem the best. Marriage, a family of my own, children. I never thought before about being a father—it seemed too far in the future. But now it feels like it would have been just around the corner for me. If it weren't for . . . tomorrow.

I'm not excited anymore. Or afraid. Just sad.

A deep, wide feeling of sadness.

Reveille. For the first time since I started training, every single one of us is out of bed before the wake-up call. Before dressing, we all go to the latrines. It's too hard to go after you have your flying uniform on—it's a jumpsuit, all one piece.

One addition to the uniform: our ceremonial swords. After a final salute from the sergeant, we put our swords back on our beds with the little boxes. As we file out of the barracks, a soldier is already collecting them. To send to our families.

Out onto the tarmac. A table is set up there, with cups of sake lined up. Time for our three toasts. I've worked this out already. The first toast is to the Emperor's shrine. The shrine on the base isn't far from the airfield itself, and beyond that, the woods where the training planes are hidden. I raise my cup like everyone else, but in my mind I toast the planes, not the shrine.

The second toast is to the Emperor himself. I picture Uncle instead. And the last toast toward our hometowns. For me, west and a little south. I can be honest about that one.

One last speech from our commanding officer. Then we gather in squads to receive our orders. "Listen carefully," says our flight lieutenant, Watanabe. He's Japanese, of course, but a pretty good guy all the same. "Last known location of the enemy ships was a hundred forty-four degrees twenty longitude east, thirty-nine latitude north. As you know, we'll be flying in three formations. Keep your speed between seventy-five and ninety kilometers per hour. Altitude, fifteen hundred meters. All planes to use the dive tactic. Do not under any circumstances break formation. Understood?"

"Hai!" we shout all together and salute him.

Just then a soldier comes running out onto the tarmac, waving a piece of paper. "Sir!" he shouts. "Wait! An important message from Military Command!"

I turn at the sound of his voice. I've got one hand on the struts, ready to climb into the cockpit. A message? It's not a normal part of the routine, as far as I know. Should we fall back into squads?

The CO reads the message. I'm pretty far away, so I can't tell from his expression if it's good news or bad. A change of enemy position, maybe? New information about their fighters?

He calls us back into squad formation.

I hustle into line. I can see everyone's faces. They don't know what's going on either.

When we're all settled, the CO waves the paper. "A personal message from His Divine Majesty! Wishing you all the strength and guidance of Heaven on your mission!"

I keep my face steady, but inside I'm rolling my eyes. Just what I need: personal encouragement from the Emperor.

We're dismissed again. I climb into my plane. It's not really mine, but that's how I think of it. And it will be mine now, all the way to the end.

Strapped in, headset on, instruments checked. Engine running, Watanabe's voice, and another sound—a strange thumping. I listen hard for a moment. Is there something wrong with my plane?

No. It's my heart, thudding hard. Stupid.

I check everything again, just to have something to do while I wait to take off.

Watanabe leads the way. I'm third in line. I love taking off. The wheels, grumbling on the tarmac. *Grumblegrumblegrumble*—and then that sound, gone. Only the engine noise left.

We circle the base once and waggle our wings. I look out the window.

The whole base, saluting us.

Saying goodbye.

29. Sun-hee

Nothing makes time go slower than waiting. And we were waiting for so many things—waiting for Uncle to come home, for the war to end, and now, worst of all, waiting to hear what would happen to Tae-yul.

The first few days were terrible. Every time I heard a car outside, I was sure it would stop at our house—that it was the army coming to tell us . . . what? That Tae-yul was in jail? Or the other—which I couldn't say even to myself.

A few days passed, then a week. Sometimes I thought I was losing my mind—that if we didn't learn something soon, I wouldn't be able to bear it. But if I couldn't bear it, what would I do? March into the military headquarters and demand an answer? Take the train and boat to Japan to find out myself? I thought about asking Tomo. His father was an important education official—perhaps he could find out something.

In the end, I did none of those things. I stared at my diary

163

for hours at a time and wrote what I could, which was only a few words.

> Uncertainty: *A flower*
> *dying for want of rain,*
> *the nearest cloud a world away.*

The weeks slowly grew into a month. It was full summer now, and so hot that I always felt dirty. Sweat made everything sticky. I found myself wishing I could take off every stitch of clothing and go around naked, the way babies did.

I walked home from school, trying not to drag my feet—I was hot and tired, but if I dragged my feet, I'd kick up clouds of road dust and get even dirtier. I rounded the corner and heard a loud noise. It took me a moment to realize that the noise was the voice of someone screaming.

I raised my head and froze in midstep.

It was my mother's voice. It was Omoni who was screaming.

I ran so fast that I nearly crashed into a soldier who was coming out of our gate. I stepped aside, frantic and panting, as he was followed by an officer in a smart uniform, and two more soldiers. When they'd passed me, I ran the last few steps to the door.

Omoni was standing in the doorway. She was holding her hands wide open in front of her, staring at the ground at her feet, and screaming.

"Omoni!" I said, trying to make myself heard. It was no use; it was as if some kind of evil spirit had possessed her.

She could only look up at me wild-eyed, then down at her feet again, still screaming. I looked down, too, and saw what was there on the ground.

A box, open where it had fallen.

A sword wrapped in cloth.

And an envelope.

I knew about these things. They'd been delivered before, to other households in the neighborhood. Delivered by the army to the family of a dead soldier.

A soldier who had died an honorable death, not one who'd been executed for treason.

Our plan had failed—mine and Abuji's. Either the authorities hadn't believed him, or the message hadn't gotten through.

Tae-yul had flown his mission.

My heart seemed to stop beating. My movements as I bent over to pick up the envelope were stiff and jerky. It had fallen face-down; I turned it over in slow motion.

The handwriting was Tae-yul's, so the words on the envelope—*To the family of the late Kaneyama Nobuo*—didn't make sense. In fact, I had to read them twice, and still they didn't make sense.

I managed to drag Omoni inside. When I gripped her arm firmly, she seemed to come to herself a little, and she stopped screaming. She let me lead her into the sitting room. I helped her sit down and hurried to make her some tea. As long as I kept busy, I wouldn't have to think about what the words on the envelope meant.

The news must have reached Abuji somehow, for he came home then, much earlier than usual. I had put the envelope on a shelf in the kitchen. Hastily, I stepped into the court-yard and handed it to him.

He opened it and read the letter right there where he stood. Then he closed his eyes for a long moment, and when he opened them again I couldn't look at him.

I followed him into the sitting room. He touched Omoni on the shoulder but said nothing; there was no need. She didn't respond at all, her face the color of ashes and her body still as a stone.

Then Abuji turned to me. He tried to speak but couldn't. Instead, he handed me the letter. My hands shook so hard that the paper rattled; I tightened my fingers on the edges to stop their trembling so I could read.

My dear family,

I am free to write whatever I wish in this letter, and I have been promised that it will not be censored. So I begin by telling you that tomorrow morning I will take part in a Special Attack Unit mission. I am a member of the kamikaze, the "divine wind" pilot corps.

I'd guessed right. But I felt no satisfaction—I felt nothing at all. I kept reading:

You may wonder how this came about. It will not be easy to explain, but you are owed my best effort. At training camp in Seoul the officers were debating whether or not to ask for Korean volunteers for a special assignment. It seemed there was a question about our bravery. Some officers did not believe that Korean men possessed enough courage to volunteer for this kind of mission.

I could not let such an insult go unchallenged. I told our commanding officer that I would volunteer for any mission, no matter how dangerous. It turned out, of course, that they were seeking volunteers for the kamikaze.

Perhaps it sounds foolish in the telling of it, but I can assure you that my decision had the desired effect. The officers were impressed and began to treat not only me but all the Korean recruits with more respect.

To be honest, we are not as well prepared as I would wish; our training was limited because of a lack of fuel and suitable equipment. You have heard of the unit's spectacular successes, but there have been many failures as well. However, I have flown a plane several times now and am confident that I will be able to do my best when the time comes. I wish for each of you the chance to ride in a plane someday; it is a thrilling and humbling experience to view the earth from above.

At a time like this it is not possible to write down everything that is in my mind. But there is one thing I wish my beloved parents to know: I am not in this position because of uncontrolled fate or misfortune. It was my choice to volunteer, and I realize that in so doing I will be leaving you without a son on this earth. I am ashamed of my decision only because of this knowledge and the pain it will cause you; were it not for that, I would go into tomorrow's mission with my heart free.

I will close this letter with a story for my sister, who so loves stories. The Japanese pilots wear special belts when they fly. These belts are made for them by the women in their families and have a special name. They are called sennin-bari—*"a thousand stitches." When a Japanese woman makes such a belt, she stands in the street with it and asks passersby to put in a stitch and wish her son or brother well as they do so. After a*

thousand people have each put in one stitch, the belt is com-
plete. The Japanese pilots believe that these belts help protect
them from misfortune because they carry the good wishes of a
thousand people.

It is a nice story, but I have no need of such a belt. When I fly
tomorrow, it will be with the assurance of my family's love, and
this alone will give me the strength to do what is necessary. My
last gift to you all is the knowledge that I have chosen the way
of my death, which is something few of us are privileged to do.

Your son and brother,
Kim Tae-yul

The letter was dated the nineteenth of June. That meant
Tae-yul had died on the twentieth, almost two weeks ago.
What had I been doing then? I refolded the letter automatically and put it back in the envelope as I tried to recall that
day. I'd have been at school—had it been sandbagging? or
bayonet practice? As long as I concentrated on trying to remember, I wouldn't have to think about Tae-yul.

We had no proper clothes for mourning, but the next day
Omoni was wearing a white mourning dress. I learned later
that it belonged to Mrs. Ahn. She had worn it in secret at the
time of her mother's passing, and then kept it hidden from
the Japanese. Omoni did not have to worry about this because the Japanese grudgingly respected those families who
had lost someone to the war effort. She drifted about the
rooms like a pale ghost.

Our grief was too deep for tears. There wasn't even a body
for us to grieve over—it was somewhere at the bottom of the
sea.

After we received that letter, the hours, the light and dark
of day and night, drifted by without any meaning. I went

about my chores, thinking only about what I was doing. This seemed the easiest way to get through the day—by talking to myself in my mind. "Let's see, we need bowls now. Five bowls—one for millet, one for beans, three eating bowls. Reach up to the shelf, get down the bowls—oops, that's only four, you need one more...."

I knew I was like a crazy person, talking to myself like that. I didn't care because most of the time it worked—it drowned out all thoughts of Tae-yul. But the knowledge of his death was like a terrible beast that lurked in odd corners of the house. In a cupboard, behind a door ... I'd be going along fine, and suddenly the fact would leap out at me, roaring, drowning out my own voice in my head: *Your brother is dead—dead—dead. . . . He will never come back—you will never talk to him or see him again, as long as you live. . . .*

And I'd stop moving and stand with my eyes squeezed shut, trembling, scarcely breathing. When the roaring stopped, I would open my eyes, dazed. Once Omoni found me in the garden, where I'd been hanging laundry. I'd frozen like that, a damp sheet in my hands, for so long that my fingers were wrinkled from the wetness.

But one afternoon in the middle of August I had to rouse myself from my dazed grief for a neighborhood accounting. I fetched Mrs. Ahn and stood in line with her. I alone was representing my family—Abuji was at work and Omoni was still in mourning dress, which meant that she shouldn't be seen in public.

I knew right away that something unusual was happening, because the block leader didn't ask us to count off. He simply waited until enough people had gathered, then made his announcement.

Not in Japanese. *In Korean.*

169

The war was over. The Emperor had surrendered to the United States.

Korea was free.

There was a brief silence, then someone shouted. Suddenly, everyone around me was shouting, throwing their arms in the air, hugging one another, laughing, crying. A man grabbed the megaphone and began singing in Korean; most of the crowd joined in. People who had not been at the accounting came out of their houses to find out what was going on and quickly joined the raucous celebration.

In the midst of that joyful commotion, I stayed quiet and felt my body begin to shake. My stomach heaved—I put my fist to my mouth and pressed hard.

Less than two months. A war that had lasted for years . . . and Tae-yul had died less than two months before it ended. I wanted to throw back my head and howl like an animal. Instead, my legs gave way and I sat down hard right there in the street.

It was old Mrs. Ahn who helped me to my feet and led me home.

30. Sun-hee

A bit at a time we pieced together what had happened. The Americans had dropped two bombs on Japan. The bombs were said to have been powerful enough to destroy half a city. At first no one could believe this. Half a neighborhood, perhaps? Or half a major military base? But Abuji eventually confirmed that half of the city of Hiroshima had indeed been destroyed on August 6, and half of Nagasaki three days later. A week later the Emperor had surrendered to the United States and its allies.

The American forces had landed in Korea to help supervise the handover of the government. And the Japanese were fleeing.

During the war there had been no battles in Korea. But now that the war was over, the fighting began. Koreans were taking their revenge on the Japanese, the Japanese were fighting back, the Americans were trying to keep order. There was chaos everywhere.

Omoni wouldn't let me leave the house. I spent a lot of time standing at the gate and watching what was going on in the street. How strange the Americans looked! They were much taller than most Koreans, with long legs and huge feet. Their faces were either so white I felt I could almost see through their skins, or so red they looked as if they'd be hot to touch. And their noses were enormous. I wondered if they could smell everything better than we could.

Abuji went into town one day soon after the Emperor's surrender to collect something called a "ration package." When he brought it home, Omoni and I crowded around him. He set it down in the courtyard. It was a dark green box that came up to my knee in height and was about a meter long. The green color was the same as the Americans' uniforms and their rumbly cars, which they called "jeeps."

The box was made of cardboard coated with a shiny substance. Whatever this was, it sealed the box so well that at first we couldn't open it. Abuji scratched the surface and examined his fingernail. "Wax," he said. "To keep out the dampness."

Omoni fetched a knife from the kitchen. Abuji scraped away at the wax until he could tear open the box.

Smaller boxes and cans and packages were inside. Omoni took them out and examined them one by one. You couldn't

171

tell what was in the cans; there was writing on them, but it was in English. There was a sack of crackers. There was even a bag of rice! Omoni drew in her breath with a whistling sound, tore open the bag and poured some rice into her hand right then and there.

It was rice, to be sure, but like none we'd ever seen before—thin grains rather than the rounded stubby ones we were used to. I almost laughed when I saw this; even American rice was long and skinny.

Abuji let out a surprised sound when Omoni handed him a carton of cigarettes. He used to smoke before the war, but I couldn't remember the last time I'd seen him with a cigarette.

There was also a small yellow package about the size of my two fingers. A sweet smell rose from it. Omoni sniffed it and handed it to me. Not smiling—she never smiled anymore—but with a kind look on her face. I opened the package to find five thin rectangles of foil.

I offered one to Abuji, but he was already smoking a cigarette. Omoni and I each took one of the rectangles. We opened the foil; there was a flat white stick inside. Omoni licked hers. "Candy," she said. "Go ahead—eat it!"

It was delicious, but there seemed to be something wrong with it. At first it grew softer, but then it became quite rubbery and though I chewed my piece for a long time, it never broke up into pieces small enough to swallow. I swallowed it anyway, and almost choked as the big rubbery lump went down my throat.

Omoni frowned and took hers out of her mouth, examining it closely. "Not for swallowing," she said. "It must be something for chewing. The way some people chew tobacco."

I learned later that the Americans called it "gum," and that

Omoni had been right—it wasn't for swallowing. For a few moments it had been a welcome distraction, but then I thought about how I wished Tae-yul were there, to share the gum with. The pleasure brought by the ration package dissolved in an instant.

How was it that even something strange and new reminded me of him?

During the next few weeks Abuji often brought home some kind of food. In town there were workers and soldiers who gave out more rations—not rice but bags of flour and beans. We were eating better than we had in years.

One day as we were finishing dinner Abuji said that the Americans were assisting with a large evacuation of Japanese civilians. I looked up from my bowl of peaches. They were from one of the ration cans—almost unbelievably luscious, cooked in some kind of sugary water.

I was sure he'd learned about this latest news from Tomo's father—that Tomo's family was among those to be evacuated.

The next day I slipped out of the house and made my way down the street to Tomo's house. He was outside loading a crate onto a cart. An American soldier was standing guard at the gate.

"Tomo."

He turned in surprise. "Keoko! What are you doing here?"

For a moment I didn't respond—I was thinking about how he'd called me by my Japanese name. We had all gone back to using our Korean names the very day the Emperor's surrender was announced. Indeed, as part of the celebration in the street that day, people had torn up their Japanese identity papers. But Tomo had been calling me "Keoko" for five years now; it would have felt strange to hear him call me "Sun-hee."

I wasn't Keoko anymore. But the part of me that was friends with Tomo would always be Keoko, and I didn't want to forget that.

"I—I heard you were leaving," I said. "I came to say good-bye."

He nodded. "We're going to Japan. To Tokyo, I think." He sounded unsure.

I realized then that Tomo was leaving the only home he'd ever known. He'd visited Japan a few times but had never stayed for very long. What must it be like for him to be moving to a country that was strange to him—a country surely broken and devastated by war? Such an uncertain future awaited him and his family.

He looked down at his feet and spoke hoarsely. "I heard about your brother. I'm sorry."

My throat closed suddenly. At home we hadn't even mentioned Tae-yul at all; to hear someone talk about him was a terrible shock. There were things I'd planned to say to Tomo, but my mind was empty now.

I reached out and put the gift I'd brought him into his hand. "Travel well," I mumbled and fled back up the road.

I'd given him back the stone—the one he'd given me the night he came to warn me about the metal raid. I hoped it would remind him of my gratitude for that night. He'd tried to help; it wasn't his fault I'd made such a terrible mistake.

Maybe it would remind him of the good times we'd had together when we were little. And it was a tiny piece of Korea, to take with him wherever he was going.

174

Every day I spent hours watching the road. It was partly out of pure greed: the American soldiers often threw gum—and one time a wonderful sweet called "chocolate," which tasted so good it made me want more. Standing at the gate also seemed to make time pass—each day was much like the one before, and it helped to be able to lose track.

Otherwise, I ended up thinking of time in terms of Tae-yul: it was so many weeks since he'd left, so many weeks since his first letter, so many days since his second . . . leading my thoughts where I didn't want them to go.

Always I was searching the road for Uncle. The war was over, the Japanese had been defeated, and there was no more need for an underground resistance. Probably he'd been somewhere far away when the war ended, which was why it was taking him so long to make his way back.

If only Uncle would come home, the house wouldn't feel so empty anymore.

It was the middle of September; a month had passed since the surrender. I heard someone call from the gate and went to meet the visitor.

I stopped partway down the path, for at the gate I could see an American soldier. I hesitated and half turned back toward the house. But Abuji wasn't home, and I couldn't very well ask Omoni to come out—she couldn't greet guests while in mourning.

The soldier called out something in English and smiled, a friendly smile. That was another thing about Americans— they all seemed to have such big white teeth. I forced myself to walk the last few steps to the gate. He handed me a parcel wrapped in brown paper. He said something else and gave me a half wave, half salute as he left. I breathed a sigh of relief that it had been such a quick visit—whatever would I have said to him?

I took the parcel into the house. It couldn't be more rations—it was flat, like a big thick envelope. On the front there was some Korean lettering. I squeezed the parcel, trying to feel what was inside. It felt like paper, many sheets of paper.

Omoni came out of the kitchen. She took the parcel and put it in the sitting room to await Abuji's return from the school.

I was in the kitchen when I heard Abuji's steps in the entry corridor. I hurried into the sitting room, fetched the parcel, and handed it to him.

He didn't open it right away. He went into the sitting room, set it down on the table, and put his things away. I stood by the door, trying not to fidget. A parcel with Korean lettering . . . maybe it was from Uncle.

Abuji opened the wrapping. A piece of paper fluttered to the floor. I darted toward him to pick it up; he leaned over at the same time and we nearly cracked heads. As he straightened, holding the paper, he looked at me a little impatiently. But he didn't ask me to leave him alone, so I stayed.

The parcel held newspapers, several of them. And the piece of paper was a letter.

"Please ask your mother to join us," Abuji said.

I was back with Omoni in less time than it took for him to refold the letter.

"It's from a Miss Lim," he told us. "I met her once, before the war. She writes that she was head of a resistance group and worked with my brother." He paused for a moment.

I pressed my lips together so questions wouldn't burst

176

out of me. Uncle! Did the letter say anything more about him?

And beneath that, another thought—a woman working for the resistance? I could hardly imagine such a thing. What did she do? Did she do dangerous things—spying, delivering messages? How exciting it must have been! And what did her family think of her?

But that wasn't as important as hearing about Uncle.

Abuji looked at the letter and continued, "She says that after my brother left here, he kept printing the newspaper. He hid in different places, but eventually things became too dangerous—the Japanese were still looking for him. The resistance underground smuggled him to Manchuria, where there was a headquarters for the movement.

"Miss Lim received word after the war ended that he would be leaving Manchuria to return to Korea. But that was the last news she had of him. She says that the Communists are making things very difficult in the north. They have seized control and are allowing no travel, except for official business."

He looked at Omoni and cleared his throat. "It is likely that my brother is there now—in the north but unable to come home. She says she will write to us again if she hears more news."

The empty feeling in the house suddenly filled up my whole body. I thought of what Omoni had said to me so long ago—that I would someday be able to forgive myself for my mistake. There were times when I thought I had, but now I felt the old guilt welling up again. Uncle wasn't coming home soon. . . . No one even knew where he was. . . .

Abuji turned and put the letter away in a chest in the

corner of the room. Then he looked at us again. "Her letter says one last thing—we may want to tell Mrs. Ahn that Uncle escaped safely all those years ago."

Mrs. Ahn?

Abuji nodded, as if I'd spoken out loud. "Do you recall the accounting just after my brother disappeared, when our home was searched? There is a secret cellar in Mrs. Ahn's garden. He hid there for two nights. She helped several other resistance workers in the same way."

Old lonely Mrs. Ahn—the Japanese never suspected her! If I hadn't felt so sad about Uncle, I might have laughed out loud.

That night I ate almost nothing of my dinner, just pushed the food around on my plate. Omoni must have noticed, but she didn't chide me. After I helped clean up, I went back into the sitting room. Abuji was looking at the newspapers. Without my asking, he handed me a few of them. As I took them, I felt a little thrill break through my despair when I thought about Uncle printing these very papers.

The articles were written in both Japanese and Korean. If they'd been in Korean only, many people wouldn't have been able to read them.

I skimmed the headlines, looking for something especially interesting. It would be good to read something, to take my mind off the emptiness inside me. . . . Here was one about the education system. That might be good; I was eager for school to begin again.

The article talked about the future for Korean students.

"It is useless to regret all the hours our young people have spent being educated in Japanese. . . . Instead, we must look to find areas of strength through which their pride and learning

can be further nurtured. Kanji, for example, is based on Chi-nese characters that have long been a source of esteemed schol-arship for our people. . . . When Korea is free at last, students should turn the dedication and knowledge acquired through learning kanji to the study of their own language and to the classical literature of our country, much of which is written in Chinese. . . ."

I'd heard these ideas before. Stunned, I looked again at the top of the article. There was no author's name given. I low-ered the paper a little and looked over the top at Abuji. Our eyes met for only the briefest moment; his face was expres-sionless and he didn't say a word.

He didn't need to. I could figure this out with no help at all.

A few afternoons later Omoni and I were in the garden weeding. My hands made the right motions of digging and pulling, but my thoughts were elsewhere.

Since we'd received Tae-yul's last letter, the death letter—that was how I thought of it—I hadn't written a single word in my diary. It was as if my mind was working fine; I could enjoy our meals these days and look forward to school start-ing again, things like that. But my heart was still empty, and I never felt like writing anything. I wondered if I ever would again.

We heard the honking of a jeep's horn from the road. The Americans seemed to like honking their horns. They used them not just in warning, to clear the road, but as a greeting, too. When two jeeps were going opposite directions on the road, their drivers honked as they passed each other. It seemed quite friendly but was also very noisy.

This time, though, the honking seemed to be coming from right outside our front gate. It kept on, loud and insistent. Omoni was still wearing her mourning dress. She looked at me and nodded toward the road.

The honking stopped, and the jeep roared off as I was fiddling with the rusty latch on the side gate. Then I heard Omoni cry out—a strange choked cry. Startled, I looked back at her—it was the first sound louder than a whisper I'd heard her make in weeks.

I saw her standing there in the vegetable patch. She threw her arms out wide in front of her, waved them wildly, and made that sound again, half screaming, half choking.

What was wrong? My heart leapt in alarm and I rushed toward her. But before I could reach her she began to move, to run toward the house.

It was as if time had suddenly stopped—as if the air had turned to water and all movement was thick and slow. Omoni, running. Me, looking first at her, and then at the house.

At Tae-yul, coming out the back door.

31. Tae-yul

It's the middle of the night, but no one in our house is asleep. Omoni feeds me a meal. Then I bathe and rest. Now I come out of my room, ready to talk.

The family is in the sitting room waiting for me. But not impatient—they'd have waited all night. Omoni brings cups of tea. She changed out of her white dress the minute she stopped hugging me, when I first arrived. Now she's wearing her old brown dress and the dragon pin, too. She looks beautiful.

180

Sun-hee is so excited! She sits next to me, then moves to sit across from me, then back again. And Abuji hugged me, too, when he first saw me. He hasn't done that since I was a small child.

I look at all of them. Smiling—I can't stop smiling. "Well!" I say. "Here I am, back from the dead.

"I want to tell you everything that has happened to me, but I hardly know where to begin. I guess I'll start with what happened after I wrote my last letter. That's a kamikaze tradition, you know. You write a letter and address it yourself—'To the family of the *late*' whatever-your-name-is. It was a funny feeling writing that. It was as if I was already dead!"

Everyone laughs. I can't remember the last time we all laughed together.

I go on. "I don't want to bore you with all the technical details, but you should know that a Special Attack plane carries very little fuel. This is because the bombs are so heavy that if the fuel tank were full we wouldn't be able to take off. They calculate the exact amount of fuel to make it to the target site—not one drop more.

"We got our orders a few days before and were waiting for the weather to clear. Finally, in the dead of night, we got the command to depart. It was still pretty cloudy that morning, but they told us the sky would clear up soon.

"They were wrong, those weather people. It never did clear up. The sky was absolutely solid with clouds, and the farther we flew the worse it got! I was in a squad with four other planes. The leader signaled to us to return to the base. There was no way we'd ever find the target in that weather."

I shake my head, remembering. "We felt so ashamed. Here we'd gotten ourselves prepared to die—the whole base had turned out to send us off. We'd written our letters and every-

181

thing. The letters had already been collected and sent—someone takes care of that as soon as the planes leave. So there we were, supposedly having accomplished this great mission, and instead we had to go skulking back to the base without even having reached the target site."

I look at Abuji. "I had a plan all along, you know. Those attacks were so difficult to accomplish. In fact, I don't know how they did it—the ones who succeeded in their missions. Most of the planes ended up getting shot down or else crashing into the ocean—missing their targets completely.

"That's what I planned to do. I'd fly out with my squad and it would look like I was attempting an attack. But I knew if I were to dive my plane just a few degrees off target, I'd miss and it would still look like I'd tried to hit it." I grin. "It would have been a double feat—I'd have done no damage to the Americans *and* I'd have taken out a Japanese plane."

Beside me, Sun-hee gasps. She's looking at Abuji. He nods at her, but neither of them says anything.

So I go on. "The clouds ruined everything. If I'd started a dive then, without any ship around for a target, they'd have known what I was up to."

I take a sip of tea. "It wasn't that I lost my nerve—" I stop again, my face growing warm. "Well, maybe a little." I can still feel it. Sitting in that plane, shaking with fear. Trying to pretend it was only the engine shaking me.

I speak quickly to get past that part. "The main thing was, if they knew for sure I was a traitor, they might make things really hard for the family. So I flew back with my squad. All that planning for nothing. And when we got back to the base we were thrown into jail for failing to accomplish our mis-

182

sion!" I shake my head again, still hardly believing it. Like the weather was our fault.

"Anyway, we were kept there for several weeks. No trial, nothing. It was like everyone had forgotten about us."

I pause for a moment. Then I stand, drop to my knees, and make a formal bow. "I apologize to my family," I say, my face still at the floor. "I realized you'd have gotten that last letter—that you all thought I was dead. It drove me crazy that I had no way of letting you know I was still alive. I apologize for the pain I caused you."

A moment's silence. Then, "There is no need for—for apology," Abuji says, his voice cracking in midsentence. I sit up again and see his face. His eyes are wet.

I clear my throat. "One day we were released, with no explanation. Eventually, we learned about the bombs, and that the Emperor was preparing to surrender. Then we were all demobilized and sent home."

Omoni lets out a long sigh. Like she's been holding her breath for years. Everyone is quiet for a few moments. No questions, not even from Sun-hee.

But it turns out she's only waiting, making sure that our parents aren't going to talk. Then, "Opah, what was it like to fly?"

I can't keep myself from grinning. "Sun-hee, you can hardly imagine it. The first time I went as a student; someone else flew the plane. I was supposed to pay attention to what he was doing, but it wasn't easy—all I wanted to do was look out the window. The houses were so tiny! And you could see the shadows made by the clouds on the ground— imagine, being higher than a cloud!

"The next few times I flew I was so busy paying attention

to the controls that I couldn't look out the window at all. There are so many things to think about—your altitude and speed, the effect of the wind, your direction, keeping the plane steady. But after a few flights I could handle the plane pretty well. So I could look out over the countryside from time to time.

"It's an odd feeling—the plane is so small inside, you're all cramped up, as if you're in a box made of metal. And the engine is very noisy. But in spite of that, you feel so free—like there's nothing but air and space around you. It's truly a miracle—you feel almost like a god."

Suddenly, I feel really tired. Abuji seems to sense it. He clears his throat. "Enough talk for tonight, my son. We should all sleep now."

He smiles broadly at all of us, longest at me. "We have plenty of time to talk in the days to come."

That hellhole of a prison . . . I haven't told them anything about that, and I won't either. There's not much to tell. It was filthy, with bad food, sometimes no food. But other than shoving a dirty dish of scraps at us once a day, the guards left us alone. Sometimes I wondered if anyone but the guards knew we were there.

I can remember lying in that cell, not sleeping much— you had to keep kicking the rats off your legs. I thought about home a lot and played games, like trying to remember every single thing in every room. Or meals—remembering all my favorite foods. Home seemed so far away. Almost like it wasn't real, like a dream.

But here I am now. Home.

Omoni's cooking. Rice again, the American stuff. It's different—it doesn't stick together the way Korean rice does, which makes it harder to eat with chopsticks. But still, it's rice.

Sun-hee's questions. Every time I see her she's asking me something—about flying or training or Japan. And I don't even mind.

But after the first few days I start to feel restless, almost like I don't belong here. How can that be? This is my home.

The trouble is, I don't know what I'm going to do. I'm busy enough for now. Abuji asked me to help at his school. Cleaning up the classrooms, repairs, stuff like that. He hopes to open it again very soon. I'm glad to help, glad to have something to do.

When the school is ready, then what? Go back to school myself? I don't feel like a student anymore. I can't see myself back in a classroom.

A job, then. But what kind of job? I'm a pilot now, and proud of it. But what good is that in a town where there aren't any planes? Not a single plane has ever landed on that airstrip.

The war was a terrible thing. But during the war I had something to do, something really important. And flying was the most exciting thing I've ever done.

Now the war is over. Everything's supposed to be better, but it isn't. Not for me.

I've been home a couple of weeks. One evening everyone is in the sitting room: Omoni and Sun-hee sewing, Abuji reading, me whittling. We get together like this almost every evening now. Funny how the war made ordinary things seem special again.

But something's wrong tonight—with me. That restless feeling. I just can't settle down. I'm whittling, but not making anything, just shaving off bits and pieces of wood.

Abuji is looking through one of Uncle's newspapers. He draws in his breath a little. "Look at this," he says. "An article openly critical of the Japanese economic policy, written at the height of the war. It actually accuses officials in the government by name." He shakes his head, admiring. "It took great courage to write and publish such an article."

Before I know it I'm on my feet. My knife and the piece of wood clatter to the floor. I'm shouting, without even thinking. "What right do you have to speak of courage?"

His face—not angry but stunned. "Tae-yul—" he begins.

I don't want to hear what he has to say. I turn my back on him and run. Out the door.

All evening I walk through town. Up and down street after street, thinking over and over: *My father is a coward.*

The years of the occupation and then the war—all the terrible things the Japanese did to us . . . and what had Abuji done? Nothing. He'd kept his head down, buried himself in his books, let the Japanese do whatever they wanted. Sure, there were times when that was the smartest thing to do, maybe the only thing to do. But there were ways to fight back, and Abuji hadn't even tried.

Not like Uncle. Uncle had done something—something big. That newspaper. I've imagined it hundreds of times. Him printing the paper in some dark basement somewhere. Fixing the press when it broke, getting the paper out when no one else could have done it.

That's what I wanted to do. Something big. I had it all

planned. It would have worked, too. Except for the weather. Damn clouds. Going back to the base in disgrace. A disgrace to the Japanese for failing in the attack. A disgrace to myself, for failing in my own plan.

Am I a complete failure? At least I didn't help them capture Uncle. That was something. But probably not, when I really think about it. Uncle is too smart. He'd never have let them catch him.

So in the end, I haven't done anything. Nothing at all.

Just like Abuji.

How can I live with a father I don't respect? And if I'm just like him, how can I live with myself?

Everyone is in bed when I get home. I tiptoe into the house. The door to my room squeaks when I slide it open. I hold my breath. No sound—no one getting up. Good. I still don't want to talk to anyone.

I don't bother to turn the light off—I know I won't be able to sleep. I lie down on my mat and stare up at the ceiling. For minutes? Hours? I don't know.

A rustle at the door: Sun-hee. She comes in without asking and stands with her arms crossed, glaring at me.

"Do you think this is what Uncle would want?" she says. Whispering fiercely, so our parents won't hear. "For you to show such disrespect to Abuji?"

I sit up abruptly. "Why does he deserve my respect?" I'm careful to whisper, too. But I can't keep the anger out of my voice. "Why should I respect a coward?"

There. I've said it out loud. My breath is coming hard now. "Do you know, sometimes I think he was worse than the *chin-il-pa!* At least they *did* something—at least they took a stand! He was like a—a worm burrowing into the ground . . . hoping all the bad things would go away! How can I respect such a man? It's hard to believe he and Uncle are from the same family!"

Sun-hee stares at me for a moment. Then she hands me a newspaper and points to something in the middle of the page. "That article there," she says. "The one about education."

I glance down at the headline. "What about it?" I'm angry at her now, too.

"*He* wrote that," she says. "Abuji."

For a moment I don't think I've heard her right. I look up at her, then down at the paper again. This time I *really* look at it.

"How do you know?" I ask.

"I just know," she says. "He said the exact same thing to me, in almost the same words. You don't have to believe me," she adds stubbornly, "but I know I'm right. I'm sure he didn't put his name on the articles because he wanted to protect us."

A long moment of silence. "He wrote this?" I whisper.

"Yes," she answers. "I've been through all the papers. Abuji started writing after Uncle left."

The whole world turns upside down. Like going into a spin in a plane—everything inside out, backward, reversed, but you still have to make your brain work.

Abuji wrote articles. For Uncle's paper.

He must have used his position at the school to obtain information, and made regular contact with the resistance so his articles could be printed by Uncle.

Suddenly, I remember the nighttime raid. It must indeed

have been his work they were looking for. He'd been in danger that night. Every night.

But he'd never shown a single sign of it. He'd gone to work, come home, studied in his room—or so I thought. But he must have been writing those articles.

And I never knew.

"Why didn't he tell me?" I'm asking myself, as much as her.

She kneels on the floor beside me. "The same reason that Uncle didn't tell *him*. It was safer that way."

"But why not now? I mean, when I got home, when the war was over—why didn't he say anything then?"

She shakes her head and speaks gently. "That isn't his way, Opah. He did what he did but felt no need to talk about it."

I look at the paper again. My eyes start to feel hot, and the print slowly goes all blurry.

32. Sun-hee

Tae-yul was up very early. I heard him rustling about and slipped out of bed to join him. "Good," he said with a smile. "I didn't want to wake you, but I was hoping you'd get up."

He beckoned me to follow him and led the way outside to the workshop area. "We have a job to do," he said. I knew what he was thinking.

Together we dragged the rose of Sharon tree from under the eaves. It was still scrawny, but it had grown and was once again as tall as I was.

"By the front door," I said. "In a place of honor."

As we worked to transplant the tree, Tae-yul asked, "Are

there any flags? I think we should fly a flag on our gate. Uncle would like that—a flag to greet him."

Uncle . . . I'd made up my mind, at last. He would hate it if I felt bad every time I thought of him. Omoni was right. I would never forget what had happened, but I *had* to forgive myself if I wanted to think of him with gladness.

"No, we don't have a flag," I said. "But I'll sew one for you to put up."

He nodded, then stopped digging and looked at me, his face serious. "I saw Uncle's shop in town. It's boarded up."

"Yes. It's been vacant all this time, but Abuji refused to sell it. He wanted to keep it for—for when Uncle comes back. . . ." For the thousandth time I wondered when that would be.

The war had changed so many things. Uncle gone, Tomo gone. Jung-shin gone, too. Her family had left town immediately after the Japanese surrender, because anyone who had helped the Japanese was in as much danger as the Japanese themselves—more, maybe. I didn't know where they'd gone; I didn't even have a chance to say goodbye to her. I hoped with all my heart that she would write to me one day and let me know she was safe somewhere.

We were quiet for a little while. Then Tae-yul said, "I was thinking of training to become a printer myself. I could run Uncle's shop for him—until he gets back."

"That's a very good idea, Opah. The press is still there, you know. They used it a lot, but then it broke and no one could fix it."

Tae-yul grinned. I knew what he was thinking: Only Uncle could fix that old press. "I helped him lots of times," he said. "Maybe I can figure it out."

190

I nodded and he went on, "The shop needs a new sign. You could paint one. 'Printing—Kim Young-chun,' that's what I think it should say." He moved one hand across an imaginary sign, indicating two lines of large lettering.

Kim Young-chun. Uncle's real name.

"Abuji might be disappointed that I don't want to become a scholar," Tae-yul continued. "I'll convince him by telling him that my being a printer will honor the work he and Uncle did during the war." He paused. "But there has always been a scholar in the family. If I am to be a printer, it'll be up to you to become the family scholar."

I frowned. Me, a scholar? Girls hardly ever became scholars. And there was so much work to be done everywhere, in our home, the neighborhood, the whole country. It was hard to imagine a time when books and studying would be important again.

Still, Tae-yul had come back from the dead. That made it seem as if anything was possible. I felt myself start to smile.

Tae-yul smiled back at me and picked up the shovel again. I took the trowel, and we continued our work side by side.

Soon we were finished putting the little tree in its place by the front door. Tae-yul fetched a bucket of water for it.

"Let's not tell Omoni about this," I said. "Let's just make it a surprise."

He agreed. After we put the bucket and tools away, I turned to him and said, "If you're going to be a printer, we have a lot of work to do."

" 'We'?" he asked. "Have you changed your mind already—do you want to be a printer, too, instead of a scholar?"

"No," I said, laughing. "Come inside, I'll show you."

I collected my diary and a pencil, went to Tae-yul's room, and sat on the floor beside him. "I've been working with Abuji for a few weeks now," I said. "I'll show you what I've learned so you can catch up, and then we can study together."

I wrote something and showed it to him. "You'll be a terrible printer if you don't know how to read and write," I said in a stern voice. But I couldn't keep the smile from my eyes.

He started to answer indignantly. "What do you mean—" Then he saw my face, stopped speaking, and glanced down at the page.

"*Ga, na, da,*" I said softly.

"*Ga, na, da,*" he repeated, his voice barely above a whisper.

The first three letters of the Korean alphabet.

We looked at them for a long moment. Then I handed Tae-yul the pencil and watched as he copied the letters in a neat row under mine.

Author's Note

"In the South [of Korea], one particular decade—that between 1935 and 1945—is an empty cupboard: millions of people used and abused by the Japanese cannot get records on what they know to have happened to them, and thousands of Koreans who worked with the Japanese have simply erased that history as if it had never happened."

—Bruce Cumings, *Korea's Place in the Sun*

I came across these lines while researching my previous books on Korea, all of which were set several hundred years in the past. For a long time the image of that empty cupboard kept appearing in my mind's eye. As I sought information for what would eventually become this book, I found that there were still bits and pieces, shreds and scraps, of stories in the cupboard. And some of them belonged to my own parents.

My parents told me many stories about their own childhoods in Korea—stories I had never heard before. My father told of receiving that gift of a rubber ball, of being forced to gather pine roots, and of having his first taste of chewing gum! My mother's best friend when she was little was a Japanese boy whose father was principal of the local elementary school; her father—my grandfather—was vice-principal. And her Japanese name was Kaneyama Keoko.

Although this book is a work of fiction, the historical events detailed in the story actually took place. Leaflets signed by U.S. general Douglas MacArthur were delivered by airdrop; the Japanese commandeered radios and metal; rose of Sharon trees were uprooted and burned by official order. And at least ten young Korean men died in service as kamikaze pilots toward the end of the war.

In addition to his 1936 Olympic gold medal, Sohn Kee Chung held the world record for the marathon for twelve years, from 1935 to 1947. In most record books, you will still find his name listed as "Kitei Son," and his nationality as Japanese. Korea participated in the Olympics under its own flag for the first time in 1948 in London; it was Sohn Kee Chung who carried that flag in the opening ceremonies. And in 1988 he lit the torch to open the Summer Olympics in Seoul.

The character of Miss Lim, briefly mentioned as the person who sent the packet of newspapers to Sun-hee's family, is based on a historical figure, Young-sin Im (a.k.a. Louise Yim). Educated by Christian missionaries, she went on to run her own school and was an active leader in the underground resistance movement. Im was the first woman ever appointed to a high post in the Korean government. Her career ended under a cloud of scandal when she was accused of corruption, a charge she vehemently denies in her autobiography, *My Forty-Year Fight for Korea*. Despite this disappointing end to her political ambitions, there is no doubt that she advanced considerably the cause of equal rights for Korean women.

One question raised in the story remains unanswered at the end. What happened to the girls who were taken away from the schoolyard the day Jung-shin's sister was granted a reprieve? The answer constitutes one of the most horrifying aspects of the war. Between 100,000 and 200,000 women from Korea and other countries conquered by the Japanese were forced to serve as "comfort women," satisfying the sexual needs of Imperial soldiers. After the war the Japanese government denied the existence of such a practice, and the women themselves were so ashamed that none of them came forward to reveal this atrocity. The truth was not revealed until 1979, and it still took nearly twenty years before the women received an apology from the Japanese government.

Tae-yul's mission is fictional, but for the account of its failure and other details of his life in the Special Attack Unit, I am indebted to two memoirs: *Kamikaze*, by Yasuo Kuwahara and Gordon T. Allred, and Ryuji Nagatsuka's *I Was a Kamikaze*. Also very helpful in my research for other parts of this book was Richard Kim's *Lost Names: Scenes from a Korean Boyhood*.

The book ends in 1945. In 1948, after three years of strife, Korea was divided along the 38th parallel, with a Communist government taking control in the north and a nominal democracy in the south. Many people like Uncle were thus separated from their families. In 1950 the Korean War broke out, and the nightmare of "Koreans killing Koreans" began on a large scale.

That war ended in 1953, but the country remains divided today. As of this writing, the first steps on a long and painful road to reconciliation have been taken. Athletes from both countries entered the stadium for the 2000 Olympic Games in Sydney, Australia, under one flag. In the same year, a few hundred families were reunited through a cooperative effort between the North and South Korean governments. I like to think that among them was a family like Sun-hee's.

Bibliography

Bigelow, Poultney. *Japan and Her Colonies.* London: Edwin Arnold, 1923.

Bishop, Isabelle Bird. *Korea and Her Neighbors.* New York: Fleming H. Revell, 1897.

*Choi, Sook Nyul. *The Year of Impossible Good-byes.* Boston: Houghton Mifflin, 1995.

Chung, Henry. *The Case of Korea.* New York: Fleming H. Revell, 1921.

Cumings, Bruce. *Korea's Place in the Sun: A Modern History.* New York: W. W. Norton, 1997.

Drake, H. B. *Korea of the Japanese.* New York: Dodd, Mead, 1930.

Eckert, Carter J. et al. *Korea Old and New: A History.* Seoul, Korea: Korea Institute, Harvard University, 1990.

* Of interest to readers age 12 and up

Frank, Richard B. *Downfall: The End of the Imperial Japanese Empire.* New York: Random House, 1999.

Howard, Keith, ed. *True Stories of the Korean Comfort Women.* New York: Cassell, 1995.

Hoyt, Edwin P. *The Last Kamikaze.* Westport, Conn.: Praeger, 1993.

*Kang, K. Connie. *Home Was the Land of the Morning Calm.* Reading, Mass.: Addison-Wesley, 1995.

*Kang, Younghill. *The Grass Roof.* Chicago: Follett, 1959.

*Kim, Richard E. *Lost Names: Scenes from a Korean Boyhood.* New York: Praeger, 1970.

Kim, San, and Nym Wales. *Song of Ariran: The Life Story of a Korean Rebel.* New York: John Day, 1941.

*Kuwahara, Yasuo, and Gordon T. Allred. *Kamikaze.* New York: Ballantine Books, 1982.

Ladd, George Trumbull. *In Korea with Marquis Ito.* New York: Scribner's, 1908.

Lee, Chang-rae. *A Gesture Life.* New York: Riverhead Books/PenguinPutnam, 1999.

Lowell, Percival. *Choson: Land of the Morning Calm.* Boston: Ticknor, 1885.

*Millot, Bernard. *Divine Thunder: The Life and Death of the Kamikazes*. New York: McCall, 1971.

*Nagatsuka, Ryuji. *I Was a Kamikaze*. New York: Macmillan, 1974.

*Naito, Hatsuho. *Thunder Gods: The Kamikaze Pilots Tell Their Story*. New York: Kodansha International, 1989.

Toland, John. *The Rising Sun: The Decline and Fall of the Japanese Empire, 1936–1945*. New York: Random House, 1970.

*Yim, Louise. *My Forty-Year Fight for Korea*. New York: A. A. Wyn, 1951.